"For a minute I almost thought we were a real family."

Abby didn't know how to respond. She didn't want to face reality. "Good night, Jack." She made a move to walk past him.

His voice was low and she barely heard his "Thank you."

She stopped. "For what?"

"I know we're just stand-ins for each other. That you and I aren't married and raising these kids, that all this is temporary. But it's so nice that it's hard to believe it's pretend."

She was moved by his words. But Jack was right—this was only temporary. She turned to go before she did something she'd regret.

He didn't move as she swept past him and into her room. He heard her shut the door and gently move away. Good thing. If she had stayed, he would've made a fool of himself and kissed her—again.

Dear Reader,

In 1993 beloved, bestselling author Diana Palmer launched the FABULOUS FATHERS series with *Emmett* (SR#910), which was her 50th Silhouette book. Readers fell in love with that Long, Tall Texan who discovered the meaning of love and fatherhood, and ever since, the FABULOUS FATHERS series has been a favorite. And now, to celebrate the publication of the *50th* FABULOUS FATHERS book, Silhouette Romance is very proud to present a brand-new novel by Diana Palmer, *Mystery Man*, and Fabulous Father Canton Rourke.

Silhouette Romance is just chock-full of special books this month! We've got *Miss Maxwell Becomes a Mom*, book one of Donna Clayton's new miniseries, THE SINGLE DADDY CLUB. And Alice Sharpe's *Missing: One Bride* is book one of our SURPRISE BRIDES trio, three irresistible books by three wonderful authors about very unusual wedding situations.

Rounding out the month is Jodi O'Donnell's newest title, *Real Marriage Material*, in which a sexy man of the land gets tamed. Robin Wells's *Husband and Wife...Again* tells the tale of a divorced couple reuniting in a delightful way. And finally, in *Daddy for Hire* by Joey Light, a hunk of a man becomes the most muscular nanny there ever was, all for love of his little girl.

Enjoy Diana Palmer's *Mystery Man* and all of our wonderful books this month. There's just no better way to start off springtime than with six books bursting with love!

Regards,

Melissa Senate
Senior Editor
Silhouette Books

Please address questions and book requests to:
Silhouette Reader Service
U.S.: 3010 Walden Ave., P.O. Box 1325, Buffalo, NY 14269
Canadian: P.O. Box 609, Fort Erie, Ont. L2A 5X3

DADDY
FOR HIRE

Joey Light

Silhouette

ROMANCE™

Published by Silhouette Books

America's Publisher of Contemporary Romance

To Nora
For lighting my way down a blind passageway
(with limo rides from MD to NY, champagne cocktails
at 10 a.m. and shopping trips to Bendel's & Bruno's)
Seriously, thank you, friend

 SILHOUETTE BOOKS

ISBN 0-373-19215-0

DADDY FOR HIRE

Copyright © 1997 by GeorgeAnn Jansson

This edition published by arrangement with Harlequin Books S.A.

Printed in U.S.A.

JOEY LIGHT

is married to her high school sweetheart and together, on a small farm in western Maryland, they raised four sons: a pilot/banker, a small business owner, a parole officer and a fireman. Joey's favorite place to write is a 156-year-old log cabin where her closest friend has made a place for her to wallow in her imagination while overlooking the Antietam battlefield. There, she climbs a ladder to get to the computer upstairs. Ms. Light loves music from Garth to Beethoven, fireplaces and full moons. Her first book was nominated for Best First Book and Best Kismet by *Romantic Times*. She loves to hear from her readers, so drop her a line! You can write to her c/o Silhouette Books, 300 E. 42nd Street, 6th Floor, New York, NY 10017.

HOW TO MAKE YOUR PART-TIME MALE NANNY POSITION A FULL-TIME DAD AND HUSBAND CAREER

by Jack Murdock

1) Take good care of your sexy boss's kids—they're her pride and joy.

2) Impress your irresistible boss with your handyman-around-the-house skills—what woman can resist a jack-of-all-trades?

3) Side with the boys on keeping a stray dog—you want them to like you, too!

4) Give your sultry boss a shoulder to lean on—she's had to be both mom and dad for too long.

5) Show her what a desirable woman she is—lots of compliments...and seductive kisses.

6) Propose a permanent arrangement!

Chapter One

The doorbell rang. Abby stopped in her tracks and groaned. She couldn't go through with it. She'd changed her mind. It was, after all, a woman's prerogative.

Sliding the cookie sheet into the oven, she popped the door shut. Pausing to twist the timer to nine minutes, she blew a wisp of hair from her eyes. He was here. The final applicant. Abby brushed cookie dough from her hands with the rooster-adorned dish towel. Untying her apron, she whipped it off and flung it over a chair back and headed toward the front of the house. Thank goodness this silly business could finally come to an end.

A thoughtful, careful woman, Abigail Margaret Roberts was not used to complying with an impulse, in this case a search for a "manny," or male nanny. She had no idea why she had followed through with this crazy idea.

Desperation, she laughed to herself. Pure and sim-

ple. With her two boys, life had become such a patch-
work when it should all have been so uncomplicated.
She had grabbed at straws. And now the last straw
was about to enter her house.

Abby had tried to call this applicant twice to can-
cel, but there had been no answer either time. Who
in this day and age didn't own an answering machine?
She would much rather have canceled this over the
phone than in person.

As was her habit, she stopped in the hallway to
check her appearance in the full-length mirror. Unruly
hair escaped her ponytail. Her cheeks were flushed
due to the heat in the kitchen. She looked a mess.
Too late to fix that now.

Each and every previous interview had been a di-
saster for one reason or another. The applicants were
simply weird, or her boys had acted up like little dev-
ils. One man had even scared the daylights out of her.
Gaunt and dark, he looked like something out of a
Dracula movie. She was ruing the day she had ever
decided to entertain such a foolhardy thought.

Yet it had all started so simply. A day off. A beautiful, sunshiny day just for herself. The boys were in
school, and it had just seemed like a great time to
putter in her flower garden or lounge around on the
porch.

Back then it was just a tiny seed of an idea when
she happened to turn on the television that afternoon
and catch a talk show all about men, from many different walks of life, who were turning out to be wonderful nannies. And since there was no longer a man
in this house...the idea had blossomed into something
more.

The door chime sounded again. Abby looked from

her disorderly reflection to her watch. Well, he was prompt if maybe a bit impatient. Turning toward the door, pulling in a determined breath, she took hold of the knob and yanked the heavy oak door open.

Instantly she was looking straight into the dark abyss of the wide-open mouth of the Tasmanian Devil. It adorned a blindingly white T-shirt that clung to a very broad chest. She looked up to the extrawide shoulders that stretched the fabric of the T-shirt.

Tilting her head back even farther, she finally caught sight of the face of the man wearing the cartoon shirt. She felt a jolt akin to touching the wrong thingamajig in the fuse box while standing in a tub of ice-cold water. Up to her knees.

He literally took her breath away.

Towering a good foot over her five-foot-four frame, he was lean, dark and handsome. Like something straight out of a fortune-teller's best conjuration.

He couldn't be the manny applicant. More like this gorgeously tanned guy was peddling leftover blacktop from a road job nearby. Abby looked past him to the street. No big, red construction truck idled at the curb.

Totally confused now, she looked back at him. His wavy mop of hair was the color of rich walnut. His cheekbones slashed across his face toward a nose that probably had been broken once. Twice maybe. Shadowy brown eyes were flecked with gold torchlight. Her gaze fell to his mouth, and when it curved into a slightly crooked smile, she felt her hormone level quickly bubble up and spill over like some unidentifiable potion in a mad scientist's beaker set over an open flame.

His mouth quirked down at one corner when he grinned. His upper lip was all but hidden by a thick mustache. Longish sideburns completed the picture of a desperado. All he needed was a cowboy hat on his head and a big black horse hitched to a rail.

"Hi." His voice was lazy. Deep and gravelly like a hundred-foot waterfall hidden way back in a canyon.

She shut her mouth with a snap and then opened it again. "Hello."

Abby was two clicks away from telling him she didn't need anything he was selling, but he could simply stand there and let her look at him as if he had a surplus of time on his hands.

And then the splendid hunk moved, holding out his huge hand. "I'm Jack Murdock. My appointment's at one with Mrs. Roberts."

No way was this guy a manny prospect. Absolutely no way! A rodeo champion. A race-car driver. A marauder, maybe. But definitely not a male nanny.

She laid her hand in his, and it was lost inside rock-hard, confident fingers. She swallowed hard, moistening her dry tongue.

"I'm Abigail Roberts." She didn't know whether to be thankful or sorry.

Her heartbeat did a ridiculous hop, skip, jump and cartwheel in her chest. At that cold realization, she nearly laughed out loud. She wasn't a teenager anymore. Why was she reacting to this man this way? She'd been around good-looking men before. Her body should show a little more decorum.

She squared her shoulders. Her good-mother sense kicked into gear. This was business. What kind of a man would show up for a job interview in a cartoon shirt and jeans?

She hesitated, but only for a moment. Best to get this over with as soon as possible.

"Come on in, Mr. Murdock." When he stepped forward, Abby's attention was drawn downward to a short shadow at his side. A dark-haired little girl in tiny bib overalls was clinging to his leg.

Jack Murdock bent down and took the child's hand. "This is my daughter, Katie. We come as a pair."

Abby's heart did another roll. The child was beautiful. She had curly, shiny hair with a crooked bow clipped above one ear. And his long, tall body made her short, round one seem even more fragile. The little girl's plump fingers were wrapped around one of his slender ones. She was so cute with those little round cheeks, huge eyes and that inquisitive look.

While Katie was satisfied to stay pressed against her daddy's faded denims, he reached down like a jolly giant and plucked her up into his arms to settle her on his hip. This brought an instant smile to the child's face. The beautiful little girl couldn't be more than two. Katie eyed Abby, sizing her up from under long lashes, her head tucked under her father's chin.

For a flash, Abby saw the little girl she had yearned for year after year and thought she had gotten over. Obviously she hadn't. The tug was strong as ever. Abby mentally reined in her unruly emotions.

"Hello, Katie. Right this way, Mr. Murdock." Abby led them to the bright, airy living room and motioned for them to have a seat.

Abby watched as he scanned the room for the sturdiest piece of furniture. Everything seemed dollhouse size next to him. He chose the sofa and sat cautiously as if his weight would crush the flowers in the linen pattern.

* * *

Jack Murdock balked inwardly. This whole idea
went against the grain. And he hadn't expected his
potential boss would be so beautiful. Hadn't antici-
pated her having the same effect on him that boiling
water would have on ice cubes. But here she was. Big
blue eyes, dark brown, almost auburn hair and lots of
it. A face like an angel's, but with a stubborn chin
that belied her soft expression.

And she was looking at him with doubt and something else he couldn't define. It had already been difficult enough applying for the job, hat in hand. Jack
was used to taking care of himself, getting things
done his way. He never had to ask for anything.

But he had to remember his number-one priority
now. And she was sitting in his lap. After months of
coping with his new situation, he had finally admitted
to himself that he couldn't be everything she needed.
And that alone was a hard thing for a man like Jack
to admit to himself. He couldn't be all his daughter
required. Katie was missing a woman in her life. Not
one merely paid to see to her basic needs. And Mrs.
Roberts, whatever her situation was, had advertised
for someone to run around-the-clock surveillance on
her boys. So here he was, wishing he were anywhere
else.

A man not used to justifying his actions or trying
to make anyone understand him, he mentally recoiled
at this entire scenario. Bending was new to him. Bar-
gaining was completely unfamiliar. Relinquishing
some independence was totally foreign. Yet when
once he would have simply stood up and called this
a mistake and headed for the door, now he waited.

An aroma wafted into the room to mix with the

light floral scent of her perfume. Peanut-butter cook-ies. The combination made his mouth water, which helped his mood.

Jack forced his attention back to the issue. "I came dressed casually because I wanted your kids to feel at home around me right away. My size alone is in-timidating enough sometimes. I hope it doesn't give you the wrong impression."

Well, it had, Abby admitted to herself, but not for long. There was something definitely endearing about the way he held his daughter and the way she so confidently clung to him, her tiny fingers fanned out over his muscled forearm. It was very clear they had spent a lot of time together. Each taking care of the other.

There was something very charming about the way he sat so guardedly on her flowered sofa, as if his weight threatened to collapse the supports. It proved he was a thoughtful man. Not an overbearing male who let things fall apart around him.

"Good idea, I suppose. The boys are out back." Abby folded her hands in her lap.

For some strange reason, she didn't want to dis-appoint this man. That realization didn't help her comportment any. "Mr. Murdock, I tried to reach you several times to save you a trip over here. I've changed my mind." She noticed him stiffen auto-matically then seem to force himself to relax once again.

She watched him, found herself wondering what his hair felt like. It looked so thick and curly. If they stood real close, would her head come just under his chin? Lordy, what the heck was happening to her?

She had to get her wayward, unexpected thoughts under control and focus on business.

"The truth is I hadn't thought the matter through enough when I set up the interviews. I was acting on a whim, which really isn't like me at all. I just think the manny situation is a little too radical for me."

His silence unnerved her. She felt foolish and embarrassed.

He began to stand, swinging Katie into his arms.

Words tumbled out. She wondered, only briefly, why she was so rattled. "A strange man around the house. Trusting my boys to— But of course, that was the idea wasn't it, to have someone here for them twenty-four hours a day, every day…and—"

"I wouldn't be a stranger in another five minutes or so." Jack waited while a few tense seconds slipped by and then figured he'd called in a bad bet. So be it. "But I can see you're reluctant to give it a shot. Too bad, though. I think it would have benefited all the kids. Katie gets a mother figure, and your boys get a…how did you put it? A male influence."

Abby focused her attention on Katie. What a precious little child. And no mom? Abby leaned forward and took one of the girl's hands. Her little fingers grabbed Abby's and held on. Life was totally unbalanced. She had always wanted a little girl, and she and Jim had tried hard for one more child. Now here was one not much more than a baby who needed a female presence in her life.

The little girl pointed to the life-size statue of a colorfully painted beagle that sat on the hearth. "Barney?"

Her dad chuckled. "No, that's not Barney, baby. It just looks like him."

Katie shook her head in denial and wiggled her fingers toward the statue. She tried to slip from her dad's grip. "'Mere, Barney. 'Mere!"

As naturally as if Katie was her own child, Abby reached for her and took her from her father's arms, her fingers brushing across his hard muscles, and set the child's little feet on the floor.

"Let me show you." Taking her hand, Abby led the child to the statue and hovered as Katie petted the cool, smooth glass and gently poked and inspected the animal until she understood. Abby hadn't realized until now how much she missed those discovery years when every day the child would uncover something new and exciting.

Smiling her gratefulness to Abby, Katie leaned over and gave the pooch a juicy smooch and then held her arms up for Abby to lift her. Taking her was Abby's first real mistake of the day.

It was like having her arms full of sunshine. Abby waited for the strong pull on her heart to subside. It didn't. The little girl was soft and smelled of powder. One small arm snaked around her neck as the other toyed with a button on her shirt, and Abby felt herself mentally sway. She had thought the old yearning had died off with so many other things. Now she knew it had only been hiding.

Jack Murdock was obviously disappointed about the withdrawal of the manny position, but he didn't discuss it further. Abby was glad he made it easy for her. He took his daughter when Abby offered her and shifted the child to a comfortable position on his hip. He turned to go.

Another chance for Abby to have a little girl around was walking out the door. His hand was on the doorknob. And she really needed to get some sort of routine for her boys set up before school was out.

He was pulling the door open.

Before she was fully aware of what she was doing, Abby's hand was on Jack Murdock's arm. "I'll tell you what. Let's talk about this some more. This is the end of May. School will be ending in two weeks. I really do have to have some sort of arrangement by then. If my contract goes through for the flower shop, I'll need someone to be here all the time. Please, sit back down and tell me some more about yourself, Mr. Murdock."

"Jack." His grin was guarded as he walked back to his seat on the couch and balanced Katie on one knee. Abby watched as his huge fingers fought to tie a bow in the tiny strings of her loose shoelaces. He had nice hands. A shiver rode her spine.

"I'm Abby. So...Jack, what do you do for a living?"

"I'm a contractor." He slid a folded envelope from his hip pocket and handed it to her. It was warm from his body. She set it on the end table. "Those are character references. I once owned a very profitable construction company. I'm thirty-five, divorced and have custody of Katie."

That he had custody spoke highly of the man. Courts just didn't hand over children to the father for no reason. "Just what do you know about raising boys?" Abby asked.

His smile came easily as he crossed his booted foot over his knee and adjusted Katie to a better balance. "Not much, other than that I just happened to have been one not too long ago."

"Why did you answer my ad?"

"It seemed like the idea fell right into my lap. I was setting up finger paints for Katie-girl, and there it was in black and white. The classifieds staring right up at me while I spread the morning paper over the table."

An image immediately formed in Abby's mind. This rough-and-tumble man down on his knees unfolding the newspaper and smoothing it across a miniature table. Placing the brightly colored pots of paint in a row along the edge next to the bowl of water. Red. Orange. Blue. Green. Yellow. Did he dive into the colors with her? Were they both laughing and covered with all shades by the end of the hour?

She cleared her brain. "So the thought of taking care of kids never occurred to you before then?"

He laughed. "Not hardly. But things change. I have to make sure that Katie has all she needs. You think your boys need a man around. I feel she needs a woman around her. A positive role model, some would call it. You can see that Katie is in one piece. She gets food when she's hungry, washed when she's dirty. That's the easy part. It's the day-to-day stuff that takes time and care. I try to be both mom and dad but, as you know, it's a stretch."

"May I ask where her mother is?"

"Out of state, last I heard. She has visitation but has never exercised that right, nor do I expect she will anytime soon."

"That's too bad."

"Not really. Most women become mothers the day their children are born. It never happened to my ex-wife."

"So you've been taking care of Katie all on your own? What about when you're working?"

"There hasn't been much of that. My attention was drawn elsewhere when my family started disintegrating." He wouldn't tell her he'd become a brooding, isolated recluse. And by the time he'd realized it, his business was almost in ashes. He'd pulled himself out of it and was now ready to get things back on track.

"My crew disbanded. I've been doing odd jobs here and there. A neighbor has been caring for Katie sometimes. I don't like this arrangement. She needs stability and consistency. And a woman's loving touch."

He sneered to himself. Something he, personally, would never need again in his lifetime.

Abby considered what he'd said. How bad could a man be with that line of thinking? He would probably be very good for the boys. And they definitely needed a gentle yet immovable force in their lives. Lately she'd found herself giving in too easily to their demands because she felt she had to make up for them not having a father.

"Do you drink or smoke?"

Again his grin was quick, his look one of toleration. Without hesitation, he answered easily. "I've been known to suck down a cold beer or two after mowing the grass and light up a good Havana late at night when I'm sitting on the porch or to keep the gnats away. But I also can grill a heck of a stackburger, toss hoops till I drop and I know all the secrets of successful fishing. I've pulled some good eating out of Molly's Hole over in Sharpsburg."

He winked at her, and Abby found the intimacy of the gesture sweep clear through her. She brushed the back of her warming neck, pushing damp curls back into the ponytail.

"Okay, this is a quiz." She smiled at him and sat back. "If one of the boys came home from school with a black eye, given to him by the school bully, how would you handle it?"

Once more, his answer was instantaneous and without doubt. And delivered with a sparkle in his eye. "I'd explain that talking is sometimes better than fighting. Then I'd take him into the backyard and teach him the good ol' sucker punch—just in case the words didn't work."

Abigail hid a smile. "Your views on homework? TV before or after?"

Jack pulled his daughter back on his lap after she slid to the floor and reached out for a china doll that sat on the coffee table.

"Television? Kids should be outside doing things. It's probably best they get their homework over with so the evening is free."

"Would you help them with their homework or expect them to figure it out on their own?"

His gaze met hers directly. "I hate homework, but I'd help to a point. I'm sure you do." He waited patiently for her to deny it. She couldn't.

"I hope this never happens, but what if you all come home from the store together and you find that one of the kids hasn't paid for something?"

"Lifted it? Easy. They take it back, apologize. All that Opie Taylor stuff. I'm an honest man, Mrs. Roberts, and I plan on raising honest kids."

If she had met this man at a party—before her bitter experience with her deceased husband, that is—she would have been fascinated by him immediately. Humor lurked in his eyes, and his easy good nature and confidence were nice to be around.

Little Katie sighed, yawned and leaned back against her dad, her eyes drifting closed. Jack shifted her so she was in a more prone position and added a little bounce with his knee. Abby didn't miss how natural the movement came to him.

Abigail let the offer roll off her tongue before she could stop it. "I have a couple of spare rooms. You could put her down on one of the beds if you like."

"Thanks." He stood up and picked up the dozing child.

Abby led the way, pausing as he headed into one of the spare rooms. Watching from the doorway, she became absorbed in the way this huge man bent, laid the little sleep-limp body down and pulled her shoes off. He glanced around the room and, finding a chair, pulled it over and jammed it against the side of the bed to keep her from rolling off. He pulled a corner of the bedspread over her.

He glanced up just in time to catch Abby staring at him. She couldn't pull her gaze from his quickly enough. What was this awareness that danced between them? Something so bright...like some bright orange sunspot. Perhaps it was simply a level of understanding about what the other was going through. A familiarity. That was all. Wasn't it?

The timer went off in the kitchen. Saved by the bell. Abby had forgotten all about the cookies. She scooted toward the back of the house, glad something had jerked her attention back to the here and now.

Jack caught up to her and wound his way through the huge house behind her, recognizing expensive Oriental rugs and Queen Anne furniture. The house smelled of lemon-scented polish and wildflowers.

He liked the way she was dressed. A white sleeveless top was tucked into her well-worn jeans. She wore white sandals that accented her tanned tiny feet. He thought those feet might just fit right in the palm of his hand. Her reddish brown hair swung in a long ponytail that reached to her belt and was tied off with a green ribbon, teasing him to touch it. He wondered what all that gorgeous hair would look like swinging free, falling around her shoulders. She smelled of honeysuckle. Jack Murdock breathed deeply.

The kitchen was bright and spacious, and Jack found himself looking around with genuine interest. There were pictures drawn by the kids pressed to the refrigerator with cartoon-character magnets. Two lunch boxes waited on the countertop to be filled. A tennis racket leaned against the wall, a few strings curled loose. A broken remote-control car was in numerous pieces on one end of the long table that sat in the center of the room. A lone daisy drooped from its perch in a jelly glass converted to vase. An apple, with one small bite taken out of it, teetered near the edge of the countertop.

Home. The word shouted at him.

Jack watched as she bent down to pull the cookie sheet from the oven. She picked up the fresh, hot cookies with a spatula and transferred them from the aluminum onto a piece of wax paper to cool. The aroma made Jack's mouth water. Her movements made his mind wander.

He appreciated the room. Like a page from *Good Housekeeping,* it was a lived-in space. Oak furniture. A long, rectangular table with claw feet was surrounded by eight ladder-back chairs. Gleaming copper pots hung in a circle over the bright orange island center. Dark green ivy grew in shiny brass pots suspended from the dark-stained wood beams overhead. The glint of silver, the glisten of china and the sparkle of crystal winked at him from the grand antique mahogany sideboard.

He had never been poor but he knew what kind of money it took to build and maintain a home like this. And what kind of care.

A glass wall looked out over the backyard. He moved to it and watched as three kids and a woman splashed around in the Olympic-sized swimming pool. Lucky kids. There was abundance in this house. And love. He could almost feel it, hanging in the air like mist after a rain. Whatever Abigail Roberts was doing, she was obviously doing it right.

When they had discussed the interview on the phone, she had revealed it was a single-parent home. Widow. But unlike his daughter, the brothers had each other.

Abby sensed a harmony. A strange addition. A man in her kitchen. It was a split thing; part of it was uncomfortable and part of it was like the scattered pieces of a puzzle falling right smack into place. His simple presence added something to the formula here. Assurance. Safety. Consistency.

Anticipation?

She cleared her throat. "Iced tea?"

"Thanks. Nice house."

She moved about the kitchen filling two tall glasses with ice. He took a chair near the end of the table, flipped it around and straddled it. When he wasn't watching her, he fiddled with the parts of the broken remote-control car.

How long had it been since he had sat in a kitchen while a woman waited on him? Or he on her? Forever, he answered his own question, silently. Absolutely forever. His ex-wife had made sure he was soured on everything that had to do with marriage and family before she fled. And up until this very minute, he hadn't missed it one bit.

Abby placed a frosty glass in front of him. He noted the extra touch of the quartered lemon wedge on the rim. Some women just had a way of doing things that made a man feel special, he decided.

Brows knit together, up to his elbows in parts now, Jack held one up. "These batteries still good?"

"I think so." She arched a brow. "It's more like the fall it took from the garage roof that caused it to stop working."

"Roof?" he questioned without looking up.

She slid into a chair opposite him. "Yeah, I know. What was it doing on the roof? It only took Nick a second to scamper up the ladder the painter left against the garage while he went to eat lunch."

Jack shook his head. Abby jumped to her own defense. "I've tried being bilocational, but it doesn't work. I was in the bathroom with Ben playing nurse to his bloody knee. Nick knew better, but he used to get on the roof with his dad from time to time, you know, cleaning rainspouts and retrieving tossed teddy bears. It's a relatively flat roof...."

"Hey, relax, no one is accusing you of anything." He chuckled and continued to toy with the loose parts. "A little glue and time might just fix this right up."

The sight of a man sitting at her kitchen table repairing something warmed her. "Nick would like that. It's his favorite toy."

Jack took a few long gulps of his tea. "That's cyclical. In a few weeks, it'll be something else."

She grinned. So he knew about those things. "Katie loses interest quickly, too, huh?"

He nodded as he held two broken pieces of red plastic together. "My folks sent her one of those new-fangled play-tripod things. For an entire week, she seemed glued to it. Now—" he motioned a hand in the air "—nothing." The two pieces he'd been holding together fell apart.

Small talk with a man. How long had it been? How much had she simply missed the company a man brings to a woman's kitchen? No, she had purposely forgotten that. After what Jim had done to her...she would never want another man in her life again. At least not her very own personal life. She pushed those specific thoughts away and let her mind wander to less painful topics.

"Do your parents live nearby?" she asked.

"No. They would be able to help me out some if they did. West Coast. Retired. They want me to come out there to live—and I might have to if things don't work out here—but I know a lot of people in this area. My reputation is already built. And I like Maryland. Where else can you find an ocean, mountains, flatland, big cities and small? The seasons are great here. When it's summer it's hot and muggy, when it's winter it's cold and icy."

She agreed. "I like Williamstown. Old, small and quiet. Yet right on the edge of several large cities. Good place to raise kids."

Restful. Eased. Feelings that Abby seldom enjoyed anymore sneaked up on her. She listened to the sound of his deep voice override the yelps and squeals and the occasional shout at the kids from her friend who was swimming with them.

He wiped his hands on his jeans. "Do you have any tools close by?"

"In the drawer behind you. Bottom one."

He set a screwdriver, electrical tape and pair of pliers on the tabletop. He talked as he worked. "I let my carpentry business fade over the last year. I went through a time of...well, never mind. I'm going to need a chance to build it back up again. Right now I can be making my contacts by phone and running out to the job site off and on, whenever you're home for the kids. I have a friend who'll be foreman on the site for me till I get things going."

She nodded. She could see his reasoning. As a manny, he would have a salary, a place to stay and meals for both him and his daughter. He would have the benefit of an almost-wife and mother without the reality of it. Katie would never know the difference. Not for a long time anyway. Ben and Nick were a different story. Yet, she thought, maybe having him move in wasn't such a far-fetched idea after all. But could she really contend with having an almost-husband around? She hunched her shoulders. He'd never be that. Just a helper.

Jack caught her staring at him. He grinned. She warmed beneath it. It did feel as if the arrangement might work. She had hatched this flighty plan for exactly that reason, with the best interest of her boys in mind. Granted, it was a little more than Big Brothers of America, but it was no real big deal. Was it?

After catching the first few words about it from the TV talk show, she had sat down and listened. It was working. Men were proving themselves very adept at the nanny role. Retired football players were doing it. Preppies putting themselves through college were doing it. Single men not wanting to get into the office grind were doing it.

And it was successful. In many different instances, it was the answer to single or distant parenting. A different kind of family was better than no family at all. In distant parenting, it was a relief to the estranged father or mother who only had certain visitation rights to know that there was a male or female influence in the house, someone to take care of what needed tending to.

Her thoughts were moving too quickly. She got up from the table and went back to the countertop. Snagging two cookies, handing him one, she walked to the wall of glass to watch the kids.

"Mr. Murdock, those two kids out there are the most important thing in the world to me. They're my life. I'm sure you understand that with your daughter. I'd be handing you my whole being, putting it in your hands, if I were to proceed with this. It's why I have to be so careful before I make a decision. The television show made it all seem so simple, but it's far from that, I assure you."

"True enough. You placed the ad. I just answered it. I don't eat little kids for lunch, and the last time I got caught slinging one of them off the steeple of the closest church, they burned me at the stake. I'll even get a note from my mother."

She laughed. "Sometimes I wonder how we find ourselves in the situations we're in. There isn't enough of me to go around." She heard metal against metal as he continued to tinker with the broken toy.

He stated matter-of-factly, "Even between the two of us, I suspect we'd be hard put to do all, see all. I don't know anyone who does."

"What are you hoping to get out of all this, Mr. Murdock?"

He sat back in the chair and examined her. Drawing some sort of conclusion, he answered. "The same thing you are, I expect. Help. More love for the kids. They can't have too much of that, you know. Someone to share the laughs and help me wipe away the tears." He scratched his back with the screwdriver. "I don't talk like this. Don't make me talk like this."

She couldn't help but laugh at him. The twinkle in his eye, the sure way he was planted at the table.

"I'll call the boys in to meet you."

Chapter Two

Abby walked to the back door, pushed the screen open and shouted over the splashing water for the boys to come in.

Jack listened to their halfhearted protests as he grabbed a few more cookies and went back to his seat at the table only a little ashamed at how many peanut-butter cookies were landing in his gut. It had been so long since he'd had anything that tasted this good.

He was indulging himself in a feeling he hadn't had in a long time: anticipation.

Abby sauntered back from the door and over to the sink, leaning a hip on the counter. "Okay, Murdock, if you can win over these boys of mine, that aren't too keen on the idea to begin with, if you can pass the ultimate test of two tough little guys who think they're taking great care of themselves and Mom just fine, then I'll give it some serious thought. Maybe trying it for the summer."

He offered a mock salute. "Can't ask for more consideration than that."

Abby's friend Mary Kay came through the door first, way ahead of the boys, and slid to a surprised halt. "Well, hello."

Jack immediately stood up and moved over to her, offering his hand. "Jack Murdock. Nanny applicant."

"Oh, yeah. Mary Kay. Neighbor." As her son, Matt, ran through the doorway, she snagged him and slowed him down. "My kid, Matt. Slow down, big guy."

Matt buried his head in a towel as he attempted to dry his mop of thick brown hair. He was straightaway followed by two blondes that, except for a difference in height, could have been twins.

In a few moments, the room seemed filled with water droplets spraying everywhere, jabbering and laughter and yards of fluffy, multicolored beach towels.

Abby moved over to them and sped up their drying process. Dropping one of the towels on the floor, she put her foot on it and backtracked it to the door, soaking up the river the boys had let in.

The youngest boy had his green turtle inner tube still stuck securely around his waist. His darker blond hair was sticking straight up toward the sky, and his lips were turning purple from the sudden change in air temperature.

"Go upstairs and change and then come right back down. I want you to meet and talk with Mr. Murdock awhile."

The oldest drew himself taller. "Oh, Mom, we were going back out to play ball."

"Later."

Above all the groans, Mary Kay propelled Matt toward the back door, getting the unspoken message.

"Nice to meet you, Mr. Murdock."

Matt protested. Mary Kay shoved a little harder. "Move it, kid. There'll be time for playing later after you take out the trash and—"

"Oh, brother, what did I do now?" he whined as the door bounced shut behind them.

"Scoot upstairs and dry off. Cookies and milk when you're back down," Abby directed.

Silence descended as the kids left the kitchen. Abby was a little amazed that she didn't feel more uncomfortable with a stranger sitting at her kitchen table. And a male one at that. She'd been hornet's-nest mad at all men for a short amount of time after finding out more and more about her husband's "other life." But she had worked her way through that as she had almost everything else: by sheer will-power.

"Do the boys play any kind of sport?"

She laughed. "Every kind. It seems like we're on the road fifty percent of the time going to this game and returning from that one. Saturdays consist of giving up a huge midafternoon chunk of time to some sort of practice or another. And, of course, as summer grows closer there's camping trips, swimming lessons, overnights with friends, birthday parties, and so on. They keep plenty busy."

The adults heard the rumble of the boys' feet as they sped down the stairs and swung into the kitchen.

"Guys, this is Jack Murdock. The last man to apply for the nanny job."

Abby could see the curiosity in their eyes as they tried to connect this man with whatever visions six-

and eight-year-olds had of a nanny. Remembering how the kids had acted up and discounted the entire situation time and time again with previous applicants, Abby was surprised when they both just gave Jack a good look over. Of course, even they had to see he was nothing like the other candidates at all.

Jack held up the fragments of the car. "So, who's the unlucky guy who wrecked this?"

"Me," Nick, her oldest son, said proudly, poking a thumb in his chest, his eyes lighting up. "But not before I got it to do a wheelie at the roof pitch. Mom had a fit."

Abigail watched Jack as he listened intently to Nick's story. He sure would be nice to have around. But then, so were German shepherds, and even they needed a lot of upkeep. This entire situation could just turn out to be a major complication. He was much too easy on the eyes. And very substantially the classic male.

Feelings she'd thought she would never succumb to again were warming her insides. She willed them to stop, but they refused.

His jeans fit perfectly. He was handsome and had a smooth way of walking, and he simply had a great body. His stomach was flat. He was a good cross between Sam Elliott and a tall Clint Black. A man that caused a woman to conjure pictures of blazing orange sunsets...wild rides on untamed stallions...the two of them wrapped in one blanket sitting near a campfire.

Abby had to admit she felt her heart slowly melting. For the first time in a long line of drawn-out, lonely days spent resenting the male species and her stupidity in dealing with it, she felt some of her pent-up anger ease.

It was almost as if she could actually feel her life-blood snaking through her veins. Hot and way too fast. She detected a quickening. A heightened awareness of her body and mind. It was like seeing everything through 3-D glasses when all her life everything had been one-dimensional.

"Have any glue?" Jack asked, a screwdriver in one hand and pliers in the other.

Nick shook his head. "Sure, but it won't do any good to stick it all back together 'cause the motor won't work anymore."

"You're sure of that?"

Nick started to affirm his train of thought but stopped short. "I guess not. But it sure looks trashed to me." He slid from the chair and ran to his room to retrieve the tube of glue.

Ben didn't miss a thing even though he refused to crack a smile at Jack. He watched him manipulate the parts to the broken toy with fascination but remained silent.

Abby realized that Jack was simulating, without trying, what he might be able to do if he became part of the household: fit the puzzle pieces back into place, strengthen some weaknesses. Take the scattered pieces of the whole and patch them together so they'd work. Maybe not perfectly, not like the original, but quite good enough.

Suddenly Abby felt pure, cold fear slide over her. This man simply stirred up too many feelings inside of her. He was too physical, too powerful, too commanding a presence. Maybe this scenario would be the best thing for Nick and Ben, but what would it do to her? She shook her head. She was a mature adult. It would only do what she allowed it to do.

Certainly she could live in the same house with this man and not make a fool of herself. Not resent him the way she had come to resent the arrogant existence of the entire male population. Unreasonable feelings, true, and ones she could deal with if she had a mind to. Up until now, it had been easier not to.

Nick came running back, dropping a misshapen tube of model glue in Jack's hand. Instead of returning to his seat, Nick stood by Jack and the two of them bent their heads over the task.

"Ben, come on over here and hold this piece against here while Nick and I use the screwdriver to set the engine back in place."

Ben, pretty used to doing what grown-ups told him to do, got down from his chair and sauntered over, pretending to be painfully bored and unimpressed.

Abby watched, fascinated, as Jack closed his big hand over Ben's little one. "Right here. Just like that."

Jack tweaked and prodded and twisted and poked. The boys patiently handed him tools and held this here and that there. Abby was amazed that they could stand still that long. Abby forced herself to load the dishwasher. She needed to be busy doing something other than watching how deftly the man's hands worked.

They were still laboring over the broken toy twenty minutes later when Katie toddled in. Her thick, dark hair was mussed, her even darker eyes were still circled with sleep and her little mouth was curled in a tiny pout. Abigail wondered at how she found her way around the strange surroundings. And she hadn't even whimpered.

"Hi, Katie." Abigail walked slowly toward her so

as not to startle her. The little girl rubbed her eyes and blinked up at her as she drew closer.

Without hesitation, Katie stretched out both arms to be lifted up. Instinctively Abby bent down and obliged her.

The moment those soft little arms crept around her neck, the little head tucked beneath Abby's chin, she was lost all over again. All the longings for a daughter, all the wishes for a little girl in starched dresses and patent leather shoes... She and Jim used to lie awake at night and talk about what it would be like to have a daughter. Pink things and lacy stuff. Frilly dresses. Bows. Pigtails. Baton lessons.

The child smelled of warm sheets and baby shampoo. A picture of those big hands of Jack's lathering this tiny head appeared in her imagination. A man had to be unique, very special to actually take the time to perform the many tasks of raising a child alone.

And this child trusted that the adults in her life would love her and cherish her and do all the right things by her. She had no way of knowing that her mother wasn't in the picture. Not yet anyway. Abby kissed her soft cheek.

That was what Jack saw when he glanced up from his conversation about camping with the boys, the repair of the car just about completed. His daughter was being happily hugged and talked to by the cool and beautiful Abigail Roberts. The picture contracted his heart.

He detected a gentleness in the way Abby soothed his daughter. Caring. He wanted this for Katie. She deserved it. She was just a toddler and relied on him to make the best decisions for her.

Regret washed over him like a bucket of ice water. Maybe he hadn't tried hard enough to save his marriage. Maybe it was all his fault. His wife had told him it was all the time. Maybe...

He couldn't afford to dwell on what-ifs. He looked at Abby. What were these feelings she stirred in him? Gratitude. Nothing else, he assured himself. The fact that his body had tuned itself into hers the minute she had yanked the door open was only the reflection of appreciation that a workable solution might be on the horizon. To think of her in any other way would be too dangerous at this point in his life.

Okay. So he was just downright attracted to her. Strongly charmed by her. That was the natural, biological way of things. But this was business. This was only for the sake of a bunch of kids that needed some strain of normalcy in their lives.

Well, maybe one one-hundredth would be for him. A little everyday, ordinary peace and contentment. And what could it hurt to have a beautiful, sweet-smelling female to brighten up his every hour? As long as he looked but didn't even *think* about touching.

Abigail sensed that Jack was watching, and she turned toward the table to see that he sat there, dwarfing it. Something strange ran through her heart. Something warm and exiting. Something promising. She held something that was vital to him in her arms, just as she was trusting him with two little somethings that were her very life.

"Someone is looking for you, Daddy."

After taking just a few more seconds to enjoy the view, he got up, walked over to them and trapped

Abby's gaze with his own. "Well, she found me, Mommy," he teased.

Just his use of the word conjured pictures. Ones that came too quickly and too brightly.

Time ticked between them. Suspended. One. Two. Three.

He took Katie when she fell forward into his arms. They stood close, Abby and Jack. Tiny white-hot sparks danced the short distance between them to heat the air. Abigail's gaze rested on the strong, muscled arms that supported the child, the wide, square hand that chucked her under her chin. She wondered what his hands would feel like on her body.

She immediately pulled her gaze away and walked to the sink to run water, rinsing this morning's frying pan before shoving it in the dishwasher. Anything to keep occupied.

Ben, assuming the need for his help was over, headed for the other room and the television. Abby was sure he had already made up his mind about a nanny and very little could change it.

Abby listened to the sound of Jack's footsteps as he returned to the table with his daughter. She liked the sound. Security. How could a near-stranger make her feel secure in her own home?

"This is Katie. Katie, that's Nick, and that guy over there, leaving, is Ben. Say hello."

"'Lo."

Nick, who had appointed himself the man of the house since Jim's death, picked up a cookie and offered it to Katie. She took it and slid down from her daddy's lap, scooted under the table and came up on the other side to sit in the chair next to Nick. Ben voiced a forced greeting and disappeared around the doorway, and Abby listened to him plop onto the sofa and click the remote.

Abby sighed. There had to be more than a dozen ways for a heart to break. Ben was experiencing all of them.

Abby locked the door on the dishwasher and twisted the knob. It looked as if Jack would be there awhile now that he had appointed himself mechanic. The machine began its cycle.

Jack's head whipped up at the low, screeching noise. "Did you lock a cat in there?"

Nick laughed and Abby asked, "What?"

"That noise."

"Oh, that. I've gotten so used to it that I don't hear it anymore."

"Mom tried to fix it, but she got stuck."

"Mr. Murdock doesn't want to hear about that, Nicky."

Jack grinned, assuring her that he did. "Turn it off. I'll have a look at it."

"Thanks." Realizing she'd just be in the way, and wanting her kids to get to know Jack, she decided to leave. "I'll be upstairs if you want anything."

She climbed the stairs to get on with the vacuuming. As soon as she heard herself humming, she stopped short. This was new. The thought of cleaning the rugs had never brought on singing before. Either this was a good sign or a very bad one.

A diversion. Something new in their lives. Katie and Jack. They were like a beautifully wrapped box placed in front of her. A gift from someone unknown. The wondering, the curiosity at what she would find once she opened the lid, was getting the better of her.

She forced the thoughts from her mind as she

plugged in the cord and stepped on the switch, bringing the machine to life. No thinking. That had been her rule for many, many months. She counted each back-and-forth motion of the vacuum wand, one, two, three, four. Keep her mind from wandering to the man below in her kitchen, five, six, seven, eight.

When she went back downstairs, completely convinced that she had only imagined the effect Jack Murdock had on her, Nick and Jack were discussing a cabin that Jack owned somewhere up north. "And when I was a kid, we used to go sleigh riding for the entire day and have huge bonfires to roast hot dogs at night. We'd be so tired, our parents had to carry us home."

And Abby felt that edge, that awakening stir inside of her again. It wasn't her imagination. It was him. Just by being who he was, he was able to wake her out of her emotional deep sleep. Even though it was the last thing she wanted. Control. She was in command of her emotions. She would rule.

They continued their chitchat about Little League and booster shots.

Abby took the clothes out of the washer and headed out back to hang them on the line. Even if she decided to give this little scene a chance, they couldn't just fall in like roommates on some nighttime sitcom. There had to be decorum. Some distance. Just the thought of a strange man in the house was more than a bit unsettling. Yet somehow Jack didn't seen like a outsider.

It was a very large house. And there was plenty of room....

Doubt toyed with her. Tested her. Tortured her. The unknown. Here it was again. For years she had lived secure in her knowledge and realization of how wonderful her life was, only then to discover that it was all a farce. A lie! Maybe she couldn't tell the difference between illusion and reality—ever! Maybe right this minute she was being duped again.

No. No way. She was suspicious now, of everything and everybody. She was much too sophisticated to let anyone pull the wool over her eyes as her husband had. She wouldn't think of it. Not right now.

The screen door banged shut as she reentered the house.

Jack's deep voice had shifted to serious and studious. "We'll let this set overnight and then try it. It might just work long enough for you to try it on a tree limb or Highway 95."

"Oh, no, you don't!" Abby instructed, unable to believe he'd just said something like that to an eight-year-old.

"Relax. Nick and I had a talk about the proper places to run these things. He's decided he doesn't want to take any more chances with this one. Especially since he won't get it back again if he does."

She relaxed. "Good." So he was one step ahead of her and maybe had handled the rule of where to play with the remote-control car better than she had.

Jack got up and walked around to Katie. He took her hands, one at a time, and brushed the cookie crumbs from them. He led her into the living room. Abby pretended to be busy selecting something from a cupboard, but her ears were tuned in.

"Mind if Katie watches cartoons with you?"

"Nope." Ben's tone was one of complete disinterest.

"She likes the Smurfs."

"They're dumb."

"The Jetsons."

"Stupid."

"Turtles?"

"They're okay."

Jack came back into the kitchen.

Nick was on his feet instantly. "Want to see the wagon I'm working on? It's pretty old."

"Lead the way." He turned toward Abby. "Just give me a holler if Katie gets restless."

Abby nodded.

Alone in the kitchen, Abby crept to the doorway and peeped into the living room. Katie was sitting next to Ben, looking up at him. Ben was perched on the arm of the sofa, swinging one leg over the side. His gaze would wander from the television to the little girl beside him without moving his head.

In a few minutes, Katie slid from the couch and walked around the room, looking at everything. Ben's baseball mitt was lying on the coffee table, and Katie poked at it. Abby watched Ben start to make a move and then decide against it. Katie went around to the wing-back chair and pulled his brightly colored book bag onto the floor. She plopped down and played with the zipper. Ben said nothing, but he kept a wary eye on her.

Abby knew, deep down in her heart, that Katie would be good for Ben. She would draw his attention away from himself and his sadness. She would force him to interact simply by existing in the same space.

And Jack would do the same for her. Even if he was never aware of it.

What were his needs? A substitute mother for his

daughter **was** obvious. But there was more. She felt it.

Okay, so hiring him as a nanny seemed the best thing to do. It still felt weird and way out of character for her. Getting beyond that would be half the battle. Change was needed. And she needed help to expand and explore. She'd turned so sour on life for so long, she desperately needed someone to push her back into it.

Jack and Nick returned to the house, Nick jumping around and jabbering. Katie ran into the kitchen at the sound of her dad's voice. Ben nonchalantly followed a few seconds later.

"A good coat of red paint and it will be as good as new."

"I hope it holds together."

"Mom," Nick groaned, "I told you I know what I'm doing. Even Jack says it's sturdy. Stop worrying."

"It's a mother's job to worry," Jack defended her.

Nick moaned again.

"It's time for us to go. Nice to have met you Nick, Ben. Hope I'll be seeing you soon. And thank you for the cookies, Mrs. Roberts. I haven't had anything that tasted that good since… Well, I haven't had anything that's tasted that good at all. Say goodbye, Katie."

She kicked her little legs and wiggled her fingers.

Ben peeled away from the wall and darted back into the living room.

Nick turned to join his brother. "See ya, Jack, and thanks for working on stuff with me."

"Anytime, buddy."

Jack paused as Abby was walking him toward the

front door and looked at her over Katie's curly head. "Nice kids. Real nice kids."

"Thank you. And your daughter is beautiful."

Jack grinned. "Sure is. She's low maintenance, too."

It would be a big step for all of them. Regrets were something she wanted nothing to do with anymore. Not when it came to the well-being of Nick and Ben. She had to be positive. She hauled the huge oak door open.

Automatically she put her hand on his arm and again found it hard and supporting. "You must know how much I want to be sure this is the right thing to do."

He nodded.

She laughed. "No guarantees, I guess."

He shifted his weight from one foot to the other. Glancing out the open door and back to her again, his face was serious. His mouth broke into that nice grin she found she watched for already. "I guess I could simply call you and ask you out to dinner," he suggested.

His eyes were clear and direct. And saw too much. If she chose to go in this direction, she'd just have to make sure it wasn't too much of an enjoyment. Business. She instilled the word in her brain. Strictly business.

"I'll call you." Abby waved goodbye to Katie.

"Or I'll call you."

Heat coiled in her stomach, sank and whispered lower. As she closed the door, she felt the instant absence of something nice.

Abby walked back into the living room. The kids were deeply involved in a hushed conversation.

Nick could contain himself no longer. "Hey, Mom. Jack said he had a real live log cabin up in the mountains. He used to go there and fish. Stayed there all by himself even when he was little. Did you see he fixed my car?" He held it tightly and then moved to place it in a safe spot on the counter as he followed his mom back into the kitchen.

"Lunch, Ben," she called. Nick was already at the table.

Abby set a heaping plate of diagonally cut peanut-butter-and-jelly sandwiches in front of all of them. Fresh, cold milk was poured into amber glass tumblers. A bowl of rippled potato chips and a plate of freshly baked cookies finished the scene.

Abby leaned over and tweaked Nick's nose. "You liked Mr. Murdock, huh?"

Nick, sandwich fisted and mouth full by now, looked at Ben and nodded in wide-eyed, solemn agreement. Ben looked away. "Yeah, he sure wasn't like the rest of those guys. Jack's okay, Ben. You just don't want him around 'cause he's not Dad."

That struck a chord. "Nah," Ben argued instantly.

"Uh-huh," contested Nick.

Ben shoved Nick, and Nick shoved Ben back.

Nick knew what buttons to press to get to Ben. "Quit being a baby!"

Ben launched himself from his chair to Nick's, his little arms and legs going as if he wanted to pummel his brother to death. A baby, indeed.

"Hey, you two, cut it out right now. Finish eating."

Ben wrestled with Nick even though Nick managed to continue eating his sandwich at the same time. Abby moved over, lifted Ben from the body of his brother and sat him sternly in his own chair. Ben continued to send stormy glances Nick's way.

Abby studied the two tough, wiry little boys. Both light haired and dark eyed like their father. Nick had Jim's stubborn chin. Ben had his wide forehead and nose. They both showed his heart and soul, which at times had been beautiful. She silently prayed neither had inherited his weakness for lying and cheating.

Nick spoke from behind his milk mustache. "He's cool, Mom. He's big. I bet he can wrestle a real long time without getting tired."

Ben continued to eat and play with his food. "I don't like him."

Nick rolled on, ignoring his little brother's statement. "And he said he likes car racing, too, just like me."

Abby busied herself cleaning the kitchen and half listening to Nick's continuous monologue while she fell deeply in thought.

"Yep, and he likes Batman and camping, too."

"I don't like him." Ben raised his voice.

"It's okay, Ben, you don't have to like him." Abby made the statement short and simple.

She hadn't seen such interest, such excitement, shining in Nick's eyes in a long, long time. This Jack Murdock was either the best con artist she had ever seen or a godsend. Whichever, something seemed to be working.

Abigail fussed at the kitchen counter and pretended to be busy. "He seems to be very nice."

Nick's keen mind reduced it to its lowest common denominator. "Is he gonna come live with us or not?"

Chuckling, Abby capped the jelly and used the

dishcloth to clean the purple stickiness from the side of the jar. Come live with us? "Maybe...but I don't know yet."

Nick's voice took on the tone of the older, know-it-all brother and son. "Mom, let's just do it. Let's do what Dad used to say. Just close your eyes and make up your mind. Jump in with both feet. Ben, you'll like him after a while."

The words stung, hummed like a wasp sinking a venom-filled stinger. How easily Nick had repeated Jim's lines word for word. How very, very much he sounded exactly like his father. How quickly the ghostly image of him appeared, standing there in the kitchen with them, that wonderful, unforgettable grin on his face. The love for his family shining in his eyes. She wondered if that love shone from his eyes when he was with... Her heart broke. Again.

For a long moment, Abby stood there, keeping her back to her family while she absorbed the blow from the good memory and the bleak realization of reality. Jim's silhouette shimmered slowly from her mind.

She picked up her own sandwich and took a seat at the table with the boys. "The movie starts at five, and you guys have to clean your rooms before we go."

Ben pouted. "I don't like him. I don't want him here."

Nick, as always, took the lead. "Be quiet, Benny. You're too young to know what's good for you anyway." Then, to his mother, he added seriously, "Mom, we need him."

Ben slid down from his chair and pushed it hard under the table. "No, we don't."

"Oh yes, we do, Benny."

"No. No. No." Ben stood straight and tall like a little tin soldier. "I don't want him here."

"Ben." It took all her strength not to run to the little kid and scoop him up in her arms. "You don't even know Mr. Murdock. You remember when you first started wearing your in-line skates? You hated them because you kept falling and skinning your knees and elbows. After a while, you loved them because you'd gotten used to them and didn't fall much anymore. Sometimes that's the way it is with people. At first you don't like them, but after they've been around a little bit, you do."

"If he comes here, I won't talk to him. I'll hate him. I'll hate him."

Both Nick and Abby watched as Ben ran from the kitchen.

"He'll get over it, Mom. We really do need him around here. Till I get bigger anyway."

Amused that her oldest son seemed to have more control on the situation than she did, Abby grinned indulgently. "Oh, do we now?"

Completely convinced, Nick continued, "Yep, you wouldn't have to get the stepladder every time you want something off the top shelf. He can lift heavy things and fix the roof himself. He said he was a carpenter. I'll just bet he can fix the car if it breaks down, too, and you won't have to call AA and then fuss while you wait for them. He can take care of all of us, Mom. I bet he'll even fix your old bike—the one Dad couldn't fix. And then you can ride with us."

"It's AAA."

Abby shook her head. She just wished that Ben held Nick's enthusiasm for the addition of the Murdocks. Then again, maybe it was Ben's tirade that would sway her toward inviting them to try the situation. Ben needed a male presence, a brick wall to run up against once in a while.

"No promises, Nicholas, but maybe we'll be able to work a deal."

"Okay. Ben will like him after a while."

Out of the mouths of babes. It was all so clear to a child like Nick. And all so cloudy and convoluted to a child like Ben. Abby drew Nick near in a hug she knew he sometimes only tolerated, being eight. But this time she didn't feel him pull away in a hurry to get outside or shy away in embarrassment for fear one of his friends might see him actually hugging his mother.

"You're growing up so fast, Nicky. I'm so proud of you and your brother. You've been a big help to me over the past few months. I love you."

"We love you, too, Mom, even if we don't say it all the time." He did peel away from her then, grabbed what was left of his sandwich and popped it in his mouth.

That's what saw her through all the bad days. The beauty of their innocence and trust.

Later that afternoon at the theater, *Angels in the Outfield* had the boys mesmerized. Abby took the opportunity to tune out and let her mind wander.

Her shop. Her very own flower shop and greenhouse. It scared the heck out of her. She was still reeling from the fact that she had decided to make the jump. And this was her first experience with a *real* job. She had gone to high school, a couple of years of college, met Jim, fallen in love and married him. Her working outside of home was never an option. First it was designing and watching over the building of their house. Then there was the decorating and deciding on the furniture and carpeting. And then she was expecting Nick, and there was never a question that she would stay home and raise him. And she loved every minute of it.

She'd been a customer in old Mr. Morrison's shop for years. She had always loved the feeling she got when she walked in the door. Beauty in the colors, pleasure in the aromas, wonder at the miracle of the blossoms. When the shop had come up for sale, the idea struck her hard and fast. It would be security for the kids' future also. They would always have their own business and maybe could expand. And it was something she would enjoy doing. If only Mr. Morrison accepted her offer. If only the deal would go through smoothly. There was nothing she could do to hurry that situation along, so she sat back in her seat and planned what she could.

Summer vacation. She'd take the boys to the seashore. Maybe Myrtle Beach. The sun would be hot and the sand would be smooth. The water would be cold, and the air would taste of salt. Seagulls would wheel in the air, landing to chase bread crumbs. The boys would be bronzed by the sun, their hair blown by the incessant seaside wind. For a week they would be free of all pressures. She would lie back in the chaise and hide behind sunglasses for a few days of mindless sunbathing.

A haze floated through her brain, spiraling upward like a spirit from a genie's bottle. The noise from the theater disappeared. She no longer heard the voices from the screen.

A strong, handsome, desirable male face swept into

her mind's eye just as it had rolled through her doorway early that very afternoon. His clear eyes were looking deeply into hers, his mouth, that sensual mouth, was smiling at her, his hand was on her arm....

She was only having these thoughts because she had been without a man for too long, she admonished herself. And for as much as she had loved Jim and then hated him, she was living in no-man's-land now.

Oh, the good memories were still there. Buried so that she had to dig them up sometimes, but there just the same. She recollected what it was like to be held in strong, hard arms. To simply lay her head on a big, broad shoulder and let someone else take care of everything. Every little silly detail.

She missed, really missed, the feeling of being loved and cherished. But she knew she'd never feel those things again. She'd never trust a man to let him get that far ever, ever again. She just couldn't. Absolutely not. No way. She had been made a fool of once. She'd trusted and been deceived. She would never let it happen again.

Abby experienced a moment of peace before reality crashed in like a dive-bomber. Her whole marriage couldn't all have been a lie—or could it? No, in his own troubled way, Jim had loved her, been a great father to the boys, a wonderful provider. Everything a woman could want in a man and then some. Too bad he'd also been a two-timing snake.

Chapter Three

The audience laughed in unison, and Abby twisted in her seat. Welcoming the distraction, she smiled as the boys looked to her to share their glee.

Up until Jack Murdock had appeared on her doorstep, looking for all the world like a character out of an old Western movie, her plan had only focused on the boys' health and well-being. But now she thought of her own needs, as well. Just having someone reliable around all the time would be an immense relief.

And why should she feel guilty for being attracted to Jack? She was a healthy thirty-year-old female. Her body ran on a biological scheme all on its own and according to nature. It was letting her know it wasn't meant to live alone. Nature had provided for procreation by dividing the species into pairs. Two by two. One needed the other. Too bad nature hadn't instilled the urge to mate for life. Oh, well. She *had* procreated. Two handsome young men. What else did a woman need in her life?

She had no time or desire to work on a relationship, now or ever. She could never trust again; of that she was sure. Never wanted to. And the knowledge that she had been hoodwinked... Well, she hadn't been able to put a word to that feeling yet. If Jim were still alive and walked into the theater tonight, she knew one thing. She was capable of delivering one heck of a black eye.

Maybe that was part of her frustration, she realized for the first time. She hadn't been able to put closure on their relationship. Jim was dead before she had found out about any of his infidelities. She'd never been able to beat him over the head with the rolling pin. Never had the chance to call him every name in the book. Had never been able to lecture and scream for hours on end, tears falling, accusations flying. Never able to attach her fury to the end of a good right hook.

Maybe if she had, her emotions would be in a healthier state. Just like Nick and Ben, who had never had a chance to say goodbye, she'd never had a chance to retaliate. It was a wound left gaping open. But like the boys, she had to find some way of leaving it behind.

She was angry. The constant buzz, the incessant whisper of it in her ear, kept the pain alive, and she was unable to put it to rest. Not only her deep-seated anger at Jim, but, she finally admitted, at herself for not being all that he needed. The guilt gnawed inside her. If only...

Without warning, an image of Jack Murdock slid into her brain. Strangely she felt secure.

Nick jerked her attention back to the movie by shaking a container in front of her. She accepted his offer, taking a handful of greasy popcorn from the oversize red-and-white-striped box and absently popped some into her mouth. Anything to get her mind off of what she was dwelling on. It was the here and now she should be thinking about, she admonished herself.

Oh, it was sinfully good. All that butter. She licked her fingers. She focused her attention on the screen and shoved her hand toward the box of dietary-deadly popcorn again, filling her fist.

Her arm bumped into Ben's just as he held up the huge cup of ice-cold cola for her to sample, and it tumbled, hitting her knee and then the floor. A giant spout of cold cola and ice shot upward and then splashed, coating all of them with brown, sticky liquid.

Luckily the audience was laughing at a scene on the big screen, because this spill struck Abigail as the funniest thing that had happened in a week. As she laughed and laughed, tension slipped from her body and mind. Catching her breath, she chortled again. Good and loud at exactly the same time the audience's noise died down. Her glee bounced merrily and very audibly across the crowd. She slid down in her seat as heads turned her way.

The boys, laughing at their mom's laughter, mopped at their shorts and bare legs with quickly shredding napkins. She felt the strain of the day slipping away like the last of the ice cubes that melted over her legs and slid toward the floor of the theater. She stifled the remainder of her laughter as she ducked her head and covered her face with her hands.

A tap on her shoulder startled her, and she looked sharply around.

A low, gravelly voice was next to her ear, then his mouth was suddenly close to hers as she turned so quickly. "You know you could be thrown out of here for causing such a disturbance."

Absolutely nothing could compare to the shock that washed over her, the primitive sexual pull that tore at her when she found her lips only a breath away from his.

Jack slid into the seat next to her, uninvited, and settled Katie on his lap.

Surprised and inexplicably pleased, she felt a warm flush start from her middle and work its way up. Abby flipped her hair away from her face and pushed her embarrassment to the back of her mind. Along with a few other thoughts.

She stared at Jack in the semidarkness. "Where'd you come from?" she whispered.

"Three rows back. I thought that was you up here but I wasn't sure until you leapt from your chair and screamed bloody murder. Katie thought you were pretty funny." He leaned forward in his seat. "Hi, boys."

One of the boys was obviously glad to see Jack. Nick crawled over his mother to offer Jack a handful of popcorn, which he happily accepted. Ben stared straight ahead at the movie.

Abby felt the electricity travel along her flesh as her arm pressed against Jack's solid, muscled forearm in the closely linked seats.

She attempted to direct Jack's attention elsewhere. "Isn't Katie just a little bit young to enjoy a movie?"

Jack looked over and down at Abby in the dim light. The effect was lethal. Like being pinned to a velvet board with red-hot, needle-pointed darts.

"Actually I wanted to see the movie. And since I didn't have an escort for the evening, Katie volunteered." He kissed his pretty daughter's cheek. "She knows how I hate to go to a movie alone."

The little girl twisted in his lap, reached out to Nick's popcorn box and filled her hand. Then she leaned forward to get a better look at Ben. Ben shifted in his seat and pretended much too much interest in the movie.

"Cute," Abby commented drolly on his smart answer. Unable to resist, she plucked Katie from Jack's knees and cuddled her on her lap. "Now, this," she continued, indicating his little girl, "is really cute."

Jack's lazy grin and powerful dark brown eyes were playing with Abigail's senses. The shadows, the proximity, the strange hum that played between them, heightened Abby's senses, sped up the blood that pulsed through her veins. He tried to adjust his long legs, but his thigh remained resting against hers simply for the lack of room.

She could only describe the feeling as...strange. And steamy. He seemed to be surrounded by an aura of...power. He exuded conviction and energy. She could almost feel the presence, like being too close to your television screen.

His long-sleeved shirt was rolled up to his elbows, exposing solid, wide forearms. His black jeans were snug, clinging solidly to his thighs, one of which leaned against hers. She couldn't have moved away if she'd wanted to. He was magnet. She was steel.

He leaned his head over next to hers. A shock of his hair fell over his forehead. "I'll take her if she's getting heavy," he whispered.

Abby murmured back, "No, she isn't."

"Can I get you some more soda?"

"No, thanks."

He was so...so nice. And considerate. She found herself daydreaming about just the two of them being there together in the dark. His arm would be around her shoulders, his fingers fiddling with her earrings. Her head would be lying on his shoulder, her fingers entwined around his other hand. Afterward they would drive to a little-known spot, high above the city, on a little-traveled lane. He would put his fingers under her chin and turn her face toward him. Their lips...

Abby looked at him sideways in the dark. He was munching popcorn, one kernel at a time, completely engrossed in the movie, while she was here beside him bewitching a movie all her own.

She had to stifle a laugh. She had to get out more often. See more people. Spend more time in groups.

The movie rolled on. Like one great big happy family, they sat through the remaining half hour. They stood, in unison with the audience, to join in the angel wave when Mel Clark was up against the most important pitch of his life, on-screen. They hooted and clapped when the Angels won the pennant. Jack and Abby exchanged glances when the Angels' Coach Knox went to the boys' house and announced he'd called social services and decided to be the boys' father. They would be a family. A little different from the norm, but a family just the same. How coincidental.

Jack and Abby exchanged looks as the audience clapped their delight in the ending.

When the lights came up and the crowd rose in

unison, Abby hefted Katie to her hip, and they all turned single file toward the aisle.

"Want me to take her?" Jack offered.

"She's okay, thanks." Katie was playing with the gold hoop at Abby's ear.

In moments they found themselves on the sidewalk outside. Jack made a note that he liked her hair down, waving free and shiny. He had a powerful urge to grab a handful of it. She was wearing shorts that showed off her shapely and lovely long legs. A loose little blouse the color of sunshine gathered over her breasts. A thin sliver of gold circled her neck.

"We're going for pizza, Jack. Can you come with us?" Nick voiced the offer even though he'd been taught it wasn't the right way to do things. He knew he should check with her before extending an invitation for someone to join them.

Jack looked at the two boys for a minute, then at Abigail. Realizing from her motherly *I'm going to bop you* look that he might be intruding, he smiled and tested her anyway. "What do you say, Mom?"

Taking a moment to make them all squirm, she finally held her hand out for them to lead the way. But instead of following her directions, Jack simply took Katie from her and set her on her little feet, walking beside Abby, making a point of moving to the street side.

His manly gesture didn't go unnoticed. What a perfectly wonderful, gentlemanly thing to do. Why would such a simple, polite demonstration make her feel so special? And why would she love feeling so distinctive? Her respect for the man rose one more notch.

Abby unconsciously reached down and took Katie's other hand. Abby and Jack adjusted their speed to accommodate the toddler. Nick danced around in front and then ran circles around them as they walked the four blocks to the pizza parlor.

Ben walked a little way ahead of all of them. Abby knew his pout routine. But this was something more. He resented, truly resented, Jack's presence with the family. She knew he had to learn to keep all the wonderful memories of his dad alive and well within his heart and then move on. Such a horrendously huge and difficult task for such a little boy.

How easily and unquestioningly Nick had accepted Jack and his daughter. Some kids had a way of making things simple. And some had a way of making life more difficult than it really was. Nick had found some way in his little heart and mind to deal with his father's death and his own misery. Little Ben was still hurting. He was lonely and aching and angry. He was unwilling to accept another male presence easily.

By the moment, Abby knew it was becoming more and more important that she go forward with her plan for a male nanny. Ben had to begin dealing with things. Put an end to his feelings so he could grow and be happy. Abigail longed for the day life would be simple again.

The restaurant was packed with people and noisy. They were led to a booth against the back wall. A jukebox played from a corner. Delicious smells of green peppers and tomato sauce rose from the kitchen.

Jack easily issued quarters for the boys to go play the video games, and Abby watched in surprise when Nick, very naturally, took Katie's hand and led her along with them.

Jack groaned contentedly and relaxed back in the booth. "Dinner's on me."

She glanced up from the red plastic menu. "Not yet, but it can be arranged." Did she just joke and bat her eyelashes? God, where did that come from? Was she actually flirting or simply enjoying being out with another adult human being?

He grinned directly at her, and her entire body responded. "Now you're cute. It's still my treat. So what's your favorite? Let me guess…pepperoni and sausage?"

She sat back and decided to play his game. Especially since he was right.

"Okay. That was blind luck. Your favorite is…hot sausage, onions, black olives and anchovies."

"Right on the mark—almost. I hate anchovies. And I'm not real sure about the onions."

"Does Katie like pizza?"

"Wait till you see. Put a slice in front of her, and she'll pick it clean just like a little buzzard. What do the boys like? Or is that a silly question?"

She shook her head. "Silly question. They eat almost everything."

The waitress arrived, and Jack placed the order for all of them automatically. "And don't forget to come back and see if the kids want dessert."

After the woman had walked away from the table, Abby leaned forward. "Dessert? After all that junk they had at the movie and on top of pizza?"

"Better than telling her I wanted a hot-fudge sundae if I can fit it in later."

Abby liked things being taken care of. It wasn't that she couldn't do it, little things like this and mountains more, but it was very, very nice to have someone else ready, willing and able to take over. And Jack was so cheerful and naturally accommodating. Besides, she realized she was still basking in the warm glow of the happy-hearted movie they had all just sat through.

The time until the pizza arrived was spent on small talk. The lack of rainfall. The cost of kids' clothes. How quickly they wore out shoes. The carnival that was scheduled to set up in Curdy's Field very soon. The kids returned, and Nick and Ben expressed their excitement about the carnival. And then for a few minutes after the pizza was placed in front of them, quiet prevailed.

This was different. The stiffness, the strangeness, the clumsiness of their meeting earlier today, wasn't present. It was almost…almost as if two old friends had run into each other and decided to share a meal. There was a comfort here that Abby would never have expected so soon after meeting someone. He had a way about him. It was that confidence with that layer of vulnerability. She wondered what Jack would be like on a date….

Date? Had she actually thought the word? In this day and age, dating wasn't the simple thing it had been years ago. She'd have to know someone pretty well before actually going anywhere with them nowadays. Just the thought of the dating process made her want to groan out loud. And besides, the very last thing she wanted was to share time with a man.

Ben, a little more relaxed now and a smidgen less reserved, argued with his brother about the movie and whether angels were real or not.

Nick was adamant. "Yep, there's angels. I've seen

them in books and on other movies. Dead people
make angels. Right, Mom, there's angels?''

"I think so.''

"Angels are stupid. They come from heaven,'' Ben
stated sourly.

"So?'' Nick asked. "What's so dumb about
heaven?''

"You can't see it, can you? You can't even tell me
what it looks like. What do angels look like, Nicky?
They all look like girls with long yellow hair and
halos and dumb stuff like that.''

Nick ignored his young brother. "Remember the
Christmas movie, Mom, the one where when a bell
rings, an angel gets his wings?''

"Sure, Nick, I remember.'' It had become family
tradition to watch that movie every Christmas Eve.

Ben challenged belligerently, "Did you hear bells
when Dad got his wings?''

"I sure did.'' Kids. Leave it to them.

Nick, tired of arguing with Ben, switched topics
and went on to ask, as only an innocent child could,
"Do you think my mom's pretty, Jack?''

Abigail blushed as bright red as the sauce and
choked on the cola she was in the process of swal-
lowing. She was further flustered when Jack stretched
over, caught her slim wrist between his fingers and
raised her arm, patting her on the back.

He made her squirm as he eyed her directly and
answered her inquisitive son. "I certainly do, Nick.
Your mother is beautiful.''

Nick nodded his head, agreeing and smiling.
"Yep.''

Katie had glued herself to Nick now and sat on a
booster seat next to him. Jack watched as Nick played

big brother and made sure she didn't get too much food in her mouth, and when she dripped the soda on her chin, he wiped it with a napkin. Brothers. What more could a little girl ask for? After a mom, that is.

Ben, sitting on the edge of his seat, swinging his feet back and forth, looked up at Jack and asked suspiciously, "Do you like to buy surprises for kids?" Again Jack marveled at the open, honest easiness that these boys possessed. He wanted his daughter to grow up feeling as free as these children did.

Jack purposefully narrowed his eyes and tilted his head back. Using the accent of a Dracula character, he winked and asked, "Do you like to get presents?"

Nick laughed but Ben simply looked him square in the eye. "Everybody does. My dad used to bring me something from every place he went. He used to fly all over the world. He even went to Australia. That's real, real far away. He brought me back a boomerang."

Jack nodded soberly, realizing this was not the time to continue to joke around. "Your dad sounds like a great guy, Ben. I'm sorry I didn't know him."

"He's dead," Ben retorted, his bravery and sadness screwing up his little face.

Taking an arrow to the heart, Jack sat up straight and glanced at Abby and then back to Ben. "I know, buddy, I'm sorry."

"Everybody always says that, but they don't mean it. And if there was really angels, don't you think he'd be here floating around the room with us?" Ben dropped his sliver of a crust back on his plate and slid from the seat, heading for the game room.

"Ben," Abby warned, "finish your pizza."

Ben increased his speed and ran off.

Still feeling sorry for the little guy's feelings, Jack put his hand on her arm as Abby leaned forward to push her way out of the booth.

"Could you let him go for now? He just needs some time."

Abby thought a minute and then sat back against the seat. "You might be right. I think I smother him too much sometimes, and other times I think I let him get away with the wrong things. I'm not sure I even know what's right anymore."

"Gut instinct. That's what's right. You know it is." Jack's eyes searched the room for Ben, and then he drew his gaze back to Abby.

A sudden camaraderie passed between them. A general acceptance that both of them were up against the odds raising kids alone. Jack felt unusual feelings stirring inside of him. Deep inside. They were something he would have to gather up and put away somewhere. He certainly couldn't continue to think of her in any capacity except professional.

Jack plowed his way through piece after piece of pizza. Abigail loved a man with a healthy appetite and felt a certain amount of satisfaction watching this guy feed that huge frame of his. His hands. Again they drew her attention. Big. Square. Tough. Competent. A shiver rode her spine. It came from nowhere and went away just as quickly. It was the thought of those hands on her body. She forced herself back to reality.

He patted his full stomach. "I see Ms. Katie likes being part of a family. A pasted-together one, but one just the same. Here's some more quarters, Nick. See if you can find Ben and give him some. Your mom and I want to talk for a while."

Nick took Katie's hand, and they went off together. To make talking a little easier, Jack slid around in the booth until he was seated closer to Abigail.

Full now and feeling a little sleepy, Abby leaned back in the seat. "It has to be difficult for a man to take on the challenge of raising a child alone. Especially a girl. Boys, well, maybe they could muck along together, being made of snakes and snails and puppy-dog tails. But little girls...all that sugar and spice and everything nice."

"It's not all hard. She's my pleasure. I can chase away the monsters in the dark, soothe over bad dreams or things that go bump in the night. I can handle all the daily routine stuff. But I can't do enough of the things a woman needs to do with a child. Things they can do better. Make bows, braid hair, sing lullabies. Bring the soft gentleness to her life."

Abby nodded her understanding. "There are a lot of different things you'll have to discuss with her. The early years will be easier. The later years will put you to the test. You'll have to be quick. She will question changes in her body later on. You'll have to explain boys. Dating. Sex. Oh, lordy, I'll have to deal with that myself soon."

He grinned. "Sex?"

She plowed him in the arm. "Talking to the boys about it, I mean. I think I dread that."

"Why?" He gestured, opening both hands palms up. "It's a perfectly natural thing. A very nice, perfectly natural thing."

His words conjured a picture Abby didn't want in her mind. She forced it away, but it left her warm and tingly.

"You're right." She shrugged. "It's just that I pictured it happening differently. I saw Jim and I having that discussion with the boys. Now it's just me and… Well, I'll jump off that bridge when I come to it."

"You'll do fine."

"I admire that you have the will and the strength to take on such a long journey alone. Sometimes I get so tired."

"It isn't the way I want it. Alone isn't good for anyone." His gaze held hers. "And by the way, it's a pleasure being here with you. We appear to be any normal family out for an evening of fun."

And they were having fun. All-American apple-pie family fun.

The restaurant was clearing out a little. The constant din of voices was down to a murmur. The loud, brassy music was tuned lower, and someone switched the music from rock to country.

What kind of magic did this man possess? What kind of a spell was he casting over Nick and even her own very sensible self? He had a lazy way of being very much in control. He had an easy presence, yet there was a look about him that threatened any danger away from him and those with him. Abby knew, just knew that nothing in the world would be allowed to get to any of them if Jack were around. They would be safe. Something she hadn't felt in a long, long time.

Detachment. That would be the key. It was obvious he would be great for Nick and almost a must for Ben, but a not-so-wonderful addition to her life. More like a major complication. If she let it be so. And she wouldn't.

Ben. Right now she saw Jack as the answer to the

boy's major problem. He would be forced to deal with Jack in every day-to-day situation. And maybe Jack's good common sense and easy humor could shed some light on his feelings that she hadn't been able to touch. Sometime during the past couple of hours she'd made up her mind. So she ought to explain her plans in more detail.

"If all goes well, I might be busy with the flower business," she began. "I put a contract on the shop on Ninth Street."

"I know old Morrison's shop. It could use some repair. I can help in that department."

"Okay. Sounds good to me. But I can't pay. Jim left me a decent insurance policy. A sizable lump sum and one of those new programs where I get a very nice income every month for the next five years, but after that it stops. Short of hitting the lottery, if the shop does go, I'll be working elsewhere to put these kids through college."

"I didn't ask for money. I offered help."

"Thank you. I'm going to need more help than refurbishing. I don't know much about making a business work. It'll all be new to me."

"Common sense and people skills. You're good with people, I can tell. You won't have any trouble."

She decided to stop dancing around the real issue and just jumped right in. "Anyway, are you still interested in being nanny to those boys of mine?"

He sat well back against the seat and eyed her squarely. The wide, crooked smile on his face gave his answer away before he spoke. "Yes."

"We'll try it, for the summer. You said you need time to build your business back up, and I need to get through the summer with as few worries as possible. We'll work at helping each other. We can re-evaluate in late August.''

"Good. I don't think Ben is going to be very high on this new arrangement.''

"No. I'm sure you've picked up on the fact that he still hasn't accepted his father's death, nor does he understand that when you die there's nothing anyone can do about it. He knows he feels anger, but not why. He knows he feels sad, but doesn't know what to do with it. Maybe you can help him understand himself a little better.''

"I'm no shrink.''

"Sometimes I feel like I'm catering to him and that only reinforces some of his negative feelings. Like the belief that his father deserted him. I'm trying to make up for it, I guess, and am probably doing more harm than good. I just don't want to see him hurt any more.''

"Katie is too little to remember her mother, but I know the day will come when all the questions will be asked. I have to have the answers by then. I surely don't have them now.''

She cocked her head and smiled at him. "To the Batcave, Robin.'' She laughed. "If only we could simply call on all the action heroes. If they only really existed and could come when we needed them, beat up all the monsters and solve all the problems. Even ours.''

"That's a thought. But until they arrive, tell me what I can do for you in this new situation.''

"Me? Well, the way I look at it, we'll both help each other with whatever it takes. I don't really need anything,'' she lied.

"Except maybe a crash course on how to tell lies

and get away with it.'' He extended his hand toward her. ''It's settled, then, and settled well. I think we'll find it beneficial to all of us. Deal.''

She slipped her hand in his and accepted his handshake, gripping firmly, trying to exude confidence. All she really succeeded in doing was raising her own blood pressure. His palm was rough, and his fingers gripped hers tightly.

She sighed and felt good that the decision was made. That was half the battle. Now to follow through, work with it.

He turned her hand over, the one he, for some reason, still held in a handshake. ''You still wear your wedding ring.''

Slipping her hand from his, she fingered the gold band. ''Somehow I haven't been able to let it go. Taking it off would be accepting his infidelity.''

When Jack raised a thick brow and settled back in his seat, she continued, ''He was killed in a car accident only three miles from the house.''

He shook his head. ''Death in any form is hard to contend with. And you're really still in mourning.''

Hardly. ''I had to see the kids through this. Two young boys that were suddenly without the most vital, most meaningful man in their lives. And without reason. There's hardly a way to make them understand. I did what I could, the preacher did what he could, the neighbors and friends...but it has to happen within themselves. I think mothers should be issued a magic wand along with the birth certificate. No matter how hard I try, I come out feeling inadequate.''

Jack shook his head. ''And what have you done to take care of yourself?''

She put up her hand, assuring him it was all right.

"I'm an adult, Jack. It's different for me. For days, weeks actually, they asked why Daddy couldn't come home again. He'd just driven down to the store to buy a half gallon of Rocky Road to go with the devil's food cake I'd baked that afternoon. Damn that cake. If I hadn't... The kids wanted to go, but I stopped them and sent them to the bathroom to scrub off the remains of their play in the mud puddles out back. Just the thought of what would have happened had I let them go is enough to send me over the edge. I could never have survived if they had been with him."

Jack reached over and squeezed her hand, but when he felt her give and then resist, he backed off. For a few seconds, he felt her shoulder lean into him and then move away.

He removed his hand. "Life can be cruel," he offered in a stern voice. He was a stranger to consolation, and evidently what he had just done was the wrong thing.

With her long hair down and slipping over her shoulders, she looked much like a child herself at this moment. New at comforting, he didn't know what to do. So he just spoke his feelings. "Let some of the weight move to my shoulders now. Even if I am only going to be your household manager, I'm a good listener. If nothing else, I'm someone to bounce your conversation off of."

Too easy. Much, much too easy. Softness wasn't in her plan. As she had grown accustomed to doing, Abby shifted her mind away from the problems. "Having help, that simple word, makes me feel better already. Let's go get the kids. It's time to head for home."

He stood up and offered his hand. She only hesitated one moment before taking it and allowing his assistance. He was a gentleman, and she was going to enjoy that part of all of this. To the hilt.

"I'll follow you back to the house and get the boys bedded down for the night. You can just go home and relax."

"That's very nice of you, but I just spent hours loafing. Tomorrow evening will be okay."

Amid the full, satisfied groans, they walked back toward the theater, Jack on the outside once again, to get their cars. She headed toward a white eight-passenger van with the blue letters Kid Kab stenciled on the side and he toward a red, sporty MR2 convertible with a child safety seat clamped tightly to the upholstery.

A glimmer of a fast, moonlit ride in the fresh, tingling night air flashed through Abby's mind. Her hair down and flying out behind her, the air rolling across her body, the feel of a tough machine vibrating beneath her.

"Nice car."

"Nice bus. You'll probably have to drive mine to work so I can have…that."

Abigail laughed. "We'll work something out. I have a sedan, but I would enjoy driving your car once in a while."

She heard the roar of his machine next to the hum of her own. Somehow it came across as a sign of the two of them working in unison to achieve the goal of loving and raising healthy kids.

She ignored the message it sent that she and Jack could probably synchronize just as well.

Chapter Four

Monday evening the rain fell softly and quietly. The gray, cloudy sky tucked the sunset away for another day. It had been a long day at work, and Abby was tired. The boys were wrestling in the living room.

She was in the middle of finishing the dinner dishes and directing the boys to leave the television show they weren't even watching. It was time to clean their rooms. She was met by the groans and laughter and thumps that assured her the wrestling match continued. She sighed and dried her hands as she walked toward the living room to add a glare to her command.

They heard her coming and tore up the stairs, knowing what was in store for them if they didn't.

At that moment, the doorbell rang and, completely against her will, Abby felt a very distinct wave of pleasure in her lower abdomen. She forced it away. That wasn't what any of this was all about. Far from it.

The dim porch light shone on two beautiful faces. Raindrops clung to Jack's thick hair and slipped off Katie's yellow rain hat.

Abby stepped aside to let them enter and stated matter-of-factly, "Bad night to be moving furniture."

"Don't have much—her crib, my bed, two dressers. I borrowed a covered-bed truck." He placed Katie down on the floor and slipped her rain gear off.

Abby showed him where the coat closet was and then motioned for them to follow her.

Jack mentally shook his head. This was bound to be tough at first. Late last night, he'd come to terms with his problem of accepting and actually seeking help. It wasn't for him, but for his daughter. Her needs. Not his. No way were these needs his.

Life could become very pleasurable, and after the past year of nothing but nastiness and misery, he was going to enjoy it. From a distance. A long, long distance. A ten-foot-pole distance. There was no way a woman, any woman, was going to be vital to him again. Under his skin? Not in this lifetime.

He was a man of action. Walking softly wasn't his style. That was something reserved for other people to do. He'd just be himself and see what happened. Katie was his first concern. And time would tell if this situation would work out. In the meantime, he'd take advantage of the opportunity and see to it that his construction business got back into full swing.

As he followed Abby up the stairs, he watched—he couldn't help it—the nice rear end that was snugged into worn jeans. She'd braided her hair, a long, thick, french braid that bobbed against her back, a blue ribbon threaded through it. Diamond chips sparkled at her ears.

He was a man. Every man looked. He had a certain respect for the lady. She was tough, but with a core of marshmallow. And he'd picked up on more, so much more. But those things were for some other man to handle. Not him.

She opened a door and indicated the space inside. "This one is yours. There's an adjoining bathroom, and on the other side of that is a small bedroom. Katie can use that, and you'll be able to hear her very easily."

As they passed the boys' rooms, Nick leapt to his feet and launched himself at Jack.

"Are you moving in?"

Jack caught him midair in a hug and ruffled his hair. "For a while."

"Yippee." Hearing a noise, Nick turned to find Katie pulling his big fire truck out from under his bed.

He jumped back down to the floor. "She can play with my toys."

"That's mighty nice of you, son. Keep an eye on her while your mom holds the door for me to bring our things in."

"All right! Hey, Benny, look who's here."

Ben wouldn't be jumping for joy like Nick, but Abby pushed that concern from her mind and followed Jack back down the stairs. She caught a whiff of some spicy aftershave and breathed deeply. Distracted briefly by the reminder that a man was moving into her house, she told herself theirs was a professional relationship. Purely business.

Later the boys and Katie came downstairs to play in the living room, the boys claiming they'd finished cleaning up.

"Katie, don't touch that. You'll break it," Nick warned.

New "big brother" Nick grabbed Katie away from the end table and the glass bowl she was about to drag onto the floor. "No, no," he repeated sternly but quietly as he hauled Katie to a place on the floor beside him to watch cartoons.

Abby put her needle and thread back into her sewing basket after testing the buttons on Ben's Sunday shirt and glanced at her youngest son from the corner of her eye.

He was perched on the edge of his father's old recliner watching TV mostly, but also observing his brother and Katie interact. Miffed would probably describe his expression. Abby welcomed any other emotion than his sadness.

The children settled to watch television before Abby sent the boys off to bed. Even after she'd tucked them in and returned downstairs, she could hear sounds from other rooms in the house. The scrape of furniture on the floor. Doors shutting and opening. Footsteps from the hallway. Grown-up male-type footsteps.

She'd offered to help unpack their few boxes, to set their things straight in the dressers, but Jack had grinned and declined. So she had offered to look after his daughter while he prepared their rooms. The sweet little one who was now fast asleep on the floor, her head propped on the worn gray floppy-eared rabbit, five minutes after the boys were off to their rooms. Abby settled back against the couch and picked up the book she'd been working at reading for the past month.

Jack came flying down the stairs just as the eleven-o'clock news was beginning. "I'm finished and I'm starving. How about I order—?"

They were asleep. His daughter and his new boss. The book Abby had been reading had slipped to the couch, her page unmarked. Long, dark lashes fanned across her cheeks, her hand tucked under her chin.

Something dark and secret from deep inside of him drifted slowly upward, grabbed hold of his gut and caused his blood to heat. He let it roll through him and then he got rid of it. Fast.

For the first time since he and Katie's mother had separated, he felt a peacefulness about the child's surroundings, her well-being. He wasn't about to let anything interfere with that. Not even a little biology going haywire. Not even a lot of chemistry doing wild things to his libido.

Abby opened her eyes to find him standing there looking. Just looking.

Embarrassed for some reason, and half-angry to feel that way in her own home, Abby muttered, "What time is it?" She answered her own question by glancing at her watch. "It's late. I've got to get up early."

"I'm going have some coffee and scrounge around for something to eat. You want anything?"

She began to uncoil from the couch. "Coffee? At this hour? Doesn't it keep you up?"

"Nothing keeps me up," he boasted as he bent over and gathered the few toys scattered across the rug and dropped them in the toy box.

"Lucky you." She moved to stand up and found she had a kink in her neck. "Ouch."

He moved over to her and, without thinking, put

his hands to her shoulders. "Slept on it wrong, huh? This will help."

Help what? she thought as his strong fingers kneaded magic into her muscles. She hadn't thought about this part. The part where it would be just the two of them after the kids were in bed. Or maybe early in the morning before they woke up.

She scooted out from under his touch. "Don't treat me too good, I'll get too used to it. Go ahead and take Katie to her bed. I'll put on a small pot of coffee and heat up some of the sloppy joe we had for dinner."

Rejected, he ignored her. "I can do that."

She turned and glared at him. "So can I." She absolutely hated that she loved the feeling of having a man to do things for again. But she couldn't stop herself from moving toward the kitchen as Jack carried Katie upstairs.

After he'd tucked Katie in bed, Jack sat down at the breakfast bar and dived into one of the two hot, fat, dripping sandwiches she had prepared for him. Delicious. The kitchen was filled with warmth and the aroma of spicy tomato sauce and strong coffee.

Midyawn, she bid him a good evening. "Good night."

"Whoa. I thought you were going to join me."

"Eating at this time of the night and right before going to bed would kill me."

"Now you sound like my mother. Come on, I don't bite."

"Your mother was a logical person." She headed out of the room.

"I'm making you feel uncomfortable."

"No. Well, yes." She paused and turned back to

him. "But it'll just take some time getting used to the new way of things. For both of us."

"That's right. So why not start by sharing a snack with me?" He licked escaping sloppy joe from the bottom of the roll.

"Because we'd end up by sharing a bottle of that pink yucky liquid for upset stomachs a little later on."

He shrugged as she disappeared around the corner toward the hallway. "If distant and businesslike is the way you want it, then that's the way you'll have it. Harder that way, though," he said, and popped the rest of the sandwich into his mouth. "Damn it," he muttered, and reached for his coffee.

Abby smiled as she made her way up the stairs, the warmth of pleasure and the ice of wariness mixing in her blood.

Summertime. The end of May. June would be here with its long, hot nights, its crystal mornings. There was nothing like it. Clear, deep blue skies, new and colorful blossoms on stems alongside the road. And crisp, warm and sweet air.

Certainly her new enjoyment, her heightened awareness of her surroundings, couldn't have a thing to do with the new man in her life. Because he was simply a team member. A part of a whole, for the time being.

Arriving home from work, Abby drove the car into the garage, turned the ignition off and pulled two grocery bags from the back seat. The boys usually listened for the car and came running out to meet her. They must be in the house with the television on very loud.

Pushing through the backyard gate, Abby stopped

dead in her tracks. She stood staring at the scene unfolding before her eyes.

Nick was there but he was so busy meticulously setting paper plates and cups out on the table, he hadn't heard her drive up. A radio played country music off to one corner. Katie sat on a patch of freshly cut green grass playing dump trucks with Ben, both kids knee-deep in a freshly dumped mound of dirt. Where had that come from?

Jack stood over the barbecue grill painting burgers with a red sauce. He wore Jim's old silly oven mitt and that ridiculous Kiss The Cook apron she had given him for Father's Day.

For just a second, her heart leapt to her throat, threatening to choke her. For just a second, time spun backward and Jim was home like in the old days. Anger shot through her as it did so often of late. It wasn't Jim. Nor would she want it to be at this point.

But it certainly smacked of a cozy little family scene. The resentment that tore through her was sudden and uninvited. She stood a few seconds trembling, reining in her feelings and grabbing for control.

It certainly wasn't Jack's fault that she resented all the things she had lost so quickly. How was he to know that stupid mitt and ugly apron would evoke painful memories?

She took a deep breath and another look at the scene unfolding before her. Tranquility.

Nick was actually participating in the preparation of a meal. He was helping Jack. Two men preparing the meal. It was sort of barbaric. Cavemen. Seeing to it that the village had meat. Abby looked around to be sure there wasn't a pile of bones in the corner of the yard where they'd butchered. She grinned. Ritualistic it might be, but whatever it took to make it work was okay with her.

She tried to ignore the little twinge she felt on the edge of her feelings, the muted, tiny hurt of being left out, the little niggle of the boys never wanting to help her so much. After all, it would all wear off. After the novelty of Jack Murdock faded as quickly as that of the high-priced electronic game did, she wouldn't be feeling alone in a crowd.

Jack looked up just then and, through the lazy, aromatic smoke, saw her standing there. She was watching and she had a strange expression on her face. He experienced a strong urge to walk to her, take the packages from her hand and pull her into his arms. *Hi, darlin', have a good day in town? The kids and I have burgers almost ready. You have time for a quick bath before dinner is ready.*

His entire body felt a secretive pull. She was beautiful and she was sexy. Funny how the body couldn't define the reasons why not to feel some things. Purposefully diverting his attention, he scraped the spatula under a burger and gave it a vigorous flip.

Watching him, Abby couldn't help but notice that everything that was female in her was pulled toward everything that was male in him. A tremor rolled through her entire body. Chemistry. It could be a stubborn, insistent detail.

Altered. Things were going to be adjusted here a lot more than she had ever thought about. But it wasn't bad, was it? She could control her urges, for goodness' sake; she was a grown woman. She could ignore the magnetic field this man seemed to have around him.

Abby pushed through it and into the house to drop

her packages on the counter even as Jack moved to assist her.

"I'm fine. I'll be out in a minute. Hey, kids."

Jack threw up his hand in a slightly distracted manner and returned to his grill. She was fine. Good. She didn't need his help. He slapped the spatula down hard on the juicy burgers and pushed. Flames leapt toward him.

Abby put the few groceries away and went through the mail. Bills, bills, always bills. Her sedan needed a new transmission, the mechanic had said. The country club wanted her to renew their membership. Yeah, right, she snorted mentally. How long did it take to get someone out of the computer? She tore the envelope to shreds.

After killing time tidying up, Abby made her way to the back of the house and put her hand on the screen door to push it open. And then stopped. Standing back a little so she could peek out and not be seen, Abby examined the play that unfolded before her on the patio.

Jack had turned over his apron to Nick, who proudly stood beside the grill and carefully did a balancing act getting the burgers to a plate. Abby's first instinct was to bolt through the door and get Nick away from the grill, but she held back. He was growing up, and she worried too much. He was protected by those silly oven mitts and he was being careful as if he had been thoroughly briefed on how to handle this situation.

Katie chased a bright multicolored ball around as it consistently bounced off the end of her foot just as she reached down to catch it. She would stumble and get up and fall backward. She was laughing and playing all by herself.

But it was Jack and Benny that made her stop short. Both were sitting on the grass, their backs leaning against the garage wall. Jack was giving soft verbal instructions to Ben, who was tossing a yo-yo out in front of him only to watch it die and flop on the ground. Jack talked him through winding it up again and tossing it out once more. And again. When the bright lime green sphere merely bounced back and popped Ben on the forehead, both males laughed and Jack slid Ben's baseball cap low over his brow.

Ben, tongue caught between his teeth, rolled the yo-yo up again. After crossing his little feet at the ankles and cocking his head to the side to listen to every instruction that Jack gave him, he pitched the globe out. It bounced viciously back, and both of them had to duck. This caused torrents of new laughter. Jack dug his fingers into Ben's ribs and tickled him mercilessly.

Nick announced, very seriously and ceremoniously, "Burgers'll be ready in a minute. Anybody who wants to eat better get to the table quick."

Ben wound the yo-yo up one more time. After listening intently and concentrating on every instruction that Jack gave him again, after watching every visible direction Jack gave with his big hands and muscled arms, Ben made one more stab at it.

He flipped his little hand over, palm up, yo-yo cradled, and pitched the round orb out and forward. To his absolute surprise and delight, it rolled out, bounced and popped back into his hand.

Ben was absolutely stunned. He whipped up onto his knees and flung both arms around Jack's neck and squeezed. Jack responded by catching the boy close to him with both of his big arms.

It took only a few seconds for Ben to shove his way out of the man's hug. Realizing what he had done clearly shook him up badly. He threw the yo-yo on the ground as if to deny any interest in it and ran over to the picnic table. Scrambling up on the seat, he hung his head, his little hands supporting his cheeks.

Abby swiped at tears that appeared suddenly on her cheeks. Poor baby Ben. And Jack. She watched as he sat there a moment, obviously saddened himself by the outcome of the event. He had so much to offer her children. A father figure. Even a temporary one was better than none. Especially with Ben being so angry right now. She knew it was too early in the new setup. Way too premature for her or Jack to expect a good result. A few months with Jack would help them grow and accept things. And they could probably all remain friends even if they broke up this nanny relationship.

At that moment, she knew she had made the right decision. If for no other reason than that Ben now could roll a yo-yo with confidence.

She had the wild urge to fling the door open and march right out to him and give him a big hug. But of course, that would be the wrong thing to do. The wrong tone to set. Better she say and do nothing. In fact, she had to pretend that she hadn't seen anything at all.

Going back upstairs, Abby changed into shorts and a blouse. She piddled around rearranging things on top of her dresser and laying out her clothes to wear tomorrow.

She reached under her bed in search of her other brown pump when her hand brushed over a shoe box. As she pulled it out, the top fell off and pictures slid to the floor. She remembered the day she had put these away.

Sitting cross-legged near the foot of the bed, she took a handful of the snapshots and sifted through them. The memories flooded over her. There were pictures of Jim holding Ben when he was only a couple of days old. Nick holding Ben. Old Christmas-card photos of the four of them. They appeared to be the all-American apple-pie family.

The wedding pictures fell in her lap. All the old aches and pains came rolling back. She went ahead and took the time to let the emotions wash over her, because she wasn't planning on coming face-to-face with the past anymore.

She was jolted from her memories by a nice, deep voice. "I thought you were coming right back out. Nick burned the burgers to charcoal, but it's good for the digestion. What do you have there?" He knelt down beside her and picked one up.

She took it from him and, gathering the photos, shrugged. "Nothing. I was looking for my shoes and came across these. I was just putting them back."

"Let me see. Now, this is good. What are you, fifteen months pregnant?"

She looked at the one he had chosen. She was carrying Ben. He'd been born about a week after that picture. She and Jim were engaging in a silly pose for one of the neighbors. Jim was pretending to stuff her incredible bulk into the car. Nick, a toddler, was standing by looking up at his absurd parents with a funny, inquisitive expression on his face.

She forgot to feel the anger. "Certainly looks that way. He was threatening to drive me across a bumpy road to dislodge the load I was carrying. Ben only weighed in at seven pounds. I don't know where all that came from."

"Certainly no sign of it now."

"Why, thank you, kind sir." Truly flattered, she grinned beneath his admiring look.

"I'll do it," he offered as he shoved the box under the bed for her.

"As far into the middle as possible. After today, I move only forward. How can I expect the boys to get on with their lives if I don't do the same?"

"But you did find a certain pleasure in looking at them. Don't push all that too far away. Denying it all won't make it dissolve."

"Things are going to get easier from here on out. You're the miracle man." And she hoped he was.

"I don't know if I can live up to that description."

He was towering over her near the doorway and then moved past her to look down at the kids playing in the backyard. She followed him to the window.

Katie was trying to climb up on the picnic bench. "She's going to hurt herself," Abby said, alarmed.

"It's just soft grass underneath. She has to learn to hold on. Besides, I have a feeling one of your boys will come to the rescue."

Even as he said it, Nick moved over to Katie and got her down. Shaking his finger at her, he must have admonished her for taking the chance. He put a toy in her hand and left her there so he could finish setting the burgers on the table.

"See." In a friendly gesture, Jack slung an arm around her shoulder.

She stiffened immediately and pulled away even though she would have liked to stay.

"Whoa there. I didn't mean anything by it. You should know that I want absolutely nothing to do with a woman in any other way than what we have going here. Business partners, friends, whatever. After what I went through in my marriage… Well, it's like being snakebit. You don't go back and see if the snake is going to bite you again."

Feeling foolish, Abby laughed at his analogy. "That bad, huh?"

"The divorce was that bad. The marriage was good for a while, but she told me I'm a complete failure as a husband…and a man. She was pretty thorough about listing all my shortcomings."

His admission caused Abby's anger to surge back to the forefront. "And she didn't have any?"

"No. Not according to her." He grinned down at her.

"You're too smart to fall for that."

"Yeah. But it makes you wonder."

"So don't. I haven't known you very long, Jack, but even I can see that you're a good man. And better than a good father. You're devoted. Your daughter worships you."

They both heard Nick's last call for dinner and turned from the window, bumping into each other. He reached out and caught her arms, laughing. He felt her tense and pull away from him. "Don't be wary of me, Abby. I don't want a relationship with a woman any more than you want one with a man."

She squared her shoulders. "I guess we both know what we want, then, don't we?"

He stopped in front of her. The air was heavy with

emotions. Bottled and banked. His and hers. Reasons. Logic. Justifications. "I guess we do."

When he stepped back, she moved forward. He caught her hand and her attention. She looked directly into his eyes and felt the full force of his magnetism. "Don't pull away from me, Abby. I'm not about to make a fool of myself a second time. Friends, remember?"

She nodded and he gestured for her to go ahead of him. She took a deep breath, then breezed down the stairs and out the door without a second look back. But she could feel his presence right behind her. She longed to feel his arms around her again. But she knew that could only lead to heartache.

Chapter Five

As Abby descended to the first floor, she was met by the sounds of the kids. She pushed through the screen door to join them. Nick was her official seater, and Abby was soon directed to the picnic bench.

She beamed at him. "Thank you, little gentleman. Now let me taste one of those burgers. They smell so good." She smiled at all the faces that looked back at her. And thanked God for each and every one.

"Did you enjoy your day?" Jack asked as he cut up Katie's hamburger and poured a pool of ketchup for her to drag the pieces through.

"Yes, I did. Tiring but good. It will be great when I can quit this temp job. The real estate guy is supposed to call me with the news about the flower shop tonight. I'm nervous. It was nice not having to be concerned about being home at a certain time or worrying about who was with the kids."

"I thought you might have enjoyed the day more knowing your kids were in good hands."

She threw a leg over the picnic bench and sat. "Like Allstate? Don't fish for compliments around here, Jack." She laughed. "You either get them or you don't. Ben, why don't you come over here and sit a little closer to me?"

Ben slid his plate across the table and climbed up on what was left of the bench beside his mom. Abby put her arm around him. He laid his head against her.

Abby was being overprotective of Ben, but Jack ignored it. It was a mother's prerogative, he guessed, but he also felt it wasn't doing Ben any good to continue to coddle him. Jack would never consider being hard on the boy, but maybe Abby needed to back off a bit.

Jack took a seat beside Katie, his long legs banging against the wood, and kept up a cheerful stream of chatter with Nick. It helped him to ignore the beautiful woman across from him. Just because he found her attractive, just because he loved the lilac scent that surrounded her, just because he looked forward to being in her company, meant nothing more than that he had been alone too long. And that he was a normal male. Not that that explained the feeling that had come over him upstairs in her bedroom. But he had shrugged it off and reminded himself of their agreement to keep their relationship to that of being in business together.

He liked it here...in the backyard, toys strewed around, a lawn mower parked nearby, the scent of grease burning off the grill, the sound of clean laundry flapping in the evening breeze. Almost like a real live family. Almost.

He shook his head. He'd do what he had to do to keep things on an even keel. Get his business back

on track. Get everyone happy. A big job. He looked
over at Ben, who was still sulking against his mother.
A big, big job.

But he would keep to the role. There were no rules.
They had to wing it. The situation was unique. No
guidelines had been set for this circumstance.

Full and content, Jack found the chaise lounge and
watched as Abby pushed Katie in the swing. Jack read
the paper as Abby climbed in the sandbox with the
kids and built sand castles. With dusk falling, the
boys dragged out the badminton set. Jack felt his eyes
drifting closed.

Abby took her racket in one hand and Katie in the
other and approached Jack. "Up. Let me have the
lounger. It's your turn to occupy these tireless little
monsters. You can chase the birdie for a while."

He pretended to groan and then, leaping from the
chair, he ran into the yard pretending the boys were
the birds and he needed to swat them into the air.
Jack ran after the boys, and they dodged him. Soon
he and Nick took up the play. Ben just ran off to the
sidelines and became engrossed in digging a hole with
a spoon to run his Matchbox cars into.

It was getting too dark to see the shuttlecock.
"Okay, you guys, everybody grab something and get
this mess into the house."

Jack, arms stretched out in front, pretended to be
Frankenstein. He scooped up lots of stuff from the
picnic table and, walking stiff legged, pretended to
run smack into Abby.

"Jack, watch what you're doing."

"Frank. Me Frank." He patted Nick on the head.
"And this is Stein. Frank and Stein. We clean up
now. Eat all the trash."

Jack made chomping noises as he pretended to eat Katie's arm. She batted at him. Jack lifted Abby's hand, and Abby screamed in mock terror and, holding Katie, ran away from him. Katie roared. Jack moved rigidly toward the girls, and they ran circles around him, taunting him, calling him names.

Frankenstein leapt upon the ladies and swept them both up in his arms and twirled them around.

"Throw them in the dungeon," Nick ordered, using a crooked stick for a sword. "The gators can have them for breakfast."

Ben moved out of the shadows, approaching slowly. He picked up a stick and ran to help Nick defend the castle.

Everyone was weak from laughing so hard. And the job was getting done. And Abby wished Jack would put her down. Her heart was beating much too fast. She liked the feel of his strong arms beneath her too much.

The newly established, pasted-together family at 12101 Brandt Street began its life together.

After dark that evening, Abby, hands shoved down into the sink filled with bubbly water, scrubbed at the last dish and set it in the other side to rinse. The back door slammed shut. She turned in time to watch Jack walk through, the laundry basket in his hands, the clothes folded and stacked neatly inside. Her heart began to melt, but she shoved the feeling quickly away.

He flashed her a boyish smile. "Getting damp out there. Thought I'd better get these in."

"Thank you." She nodded toward the kitchen table. "Just set it over there."

He plunked the basket down and moved over to where she rinsed the last dish, turned and leaned back on the counter. He was very close. He smelled of fresh air. His hair was windblown. She felt the strong urge to run her hands through it.

"Want me to dry?" He'd never once been interested in drying dishes before.

She'd never turned down an offer before. "No, thanks, go ahead and get the boys pointed toward the tub. They take it together provided they don't get too rambunctious."

He hesitated for just one moment. He wanted to lean to the right. Feel her skin against his. He felt that strange pull again. As if something tying them together was drawing them closer. Inch by inch. Slowly. Drawing out the mystery. Almost touching. Magnetism. He cleared that word from his mind and replaced it with another: stupidity.

He silently laughed at that one. He had been in this situation before. Granted, not exactly like this—the two women were different, but one close, just the same. And he had moved from day to day, in a normal routine. But Pat had told him it wasn't enough. Not anymore.

Abby felt his gaze on her. A warmth started at her knees and worked its way up like mercury in a thermometer on a 110-degree day. Why didn't he go into the other room and start rounding up the kids? Why did she want him to stay a little longer?

This was different than anything she had ever felt being around Jim. Even in the beginning. Jack had a certain honesty about him, an openness that Jim never possessed. Maybe she had been wrong to swear off all men. No, no, she reassured herself, she was right.

If she only relied on herself, then she was sure to know when she was going to be let down. No surprises. No disappointments.

Crash! The sound of wood hitting wood and then glass breaking had Jack and Abby running toward the living room.

Mad at herself for standing at the sink enjoying the new help, furious that the new help was standing at the sink with her when he should have been with the kids, and seething that she couldn't be everywhere at once, Abby let her anger fly. "Oh, what now!"

She and Jack were able to see that all kids were safe and sound even if the table lamp had been knocked over and the lightbulb smashed as they ran into the room.

They all looked up at her silently, big eyes waiting.

She stood over all of them, her hands on her hips. "I've told you no roughhousing in the living room a hundred times. Now look what's happened." They could have been hurt. Hit on the head by the lamp. Cut by the glass. Knocked unconscious.

Nick was still on all fours and Katie was on his back riding horsey. Ben was closest to the mess, an afghan in his hands that he had been using as a cape, tempting the horsey to plow through it like a bull.

"Get up." She walked over and plucked Katie from Nick's back. "Get upstairs and into the bathtub, and I don't want to hear one word from either of you."

As soon as the boys were out of earshot, she whirled on Jack. "And where were you? This is part of your job, you know. If you had been watching the kids instead of..."

Instead of watching me. Abby caught something dark and dangerous flash in his eyes then disappear.

"We didn't mean it, Mom," Ben ventured from the top of the stairs. "You don't have to yell at us in front of him."

Her heart sank and her anger abated as quickly as it had sprung up. She was so used to putting a guilt trip on herself for everything that happened. So used to blaming herself even when accidents happened that she had lashed out with her tongue. She was still so uptight that maybe even a dozen days into this new situation wouldn't help. She needed to work on herself before she could work on the kids.

Jack silently headed back toward the kitchen to get the broom and dustpan. Damn it. He knew Abby was overreacting. Yelling wasn't going to help. It was an accident. They would be told. They would be reminded to play in the playroom. They would sit down and help repair the lamp even if it was never used again. Why was Abby acting as if it was the end of the world?

When he returned to the living room, Abby had disappeared upstairs with Katie. Just as well, he thought, after her outburst. But, he wondered, who was really the target of her anger: the kids, him—or herself?

As she bathed the three children, Abby smoothed over her harsh words with them but kept stern about disobeying and what could happen because of it. She put them to bed, then went to her bedroom and changed to her long, pink cotton gown before heading to the kitchen to heat some tea.

The real estate salesman hadn't called. That irritated her. She was making an offer below the asking price, but she was paying cash. She knew it would take a large sum from the insurance settlement, but it was an investment. One she would have to make work for her. Without a huge monthly payment, she figured she could do the remodeling and continue to stock without much problem.

It was only ten, but the house was dark. She padded along the familiar passageways until she found herself in the huge kitchen. Walking to the counter, she flipped on the soft lamplight.

Moving to the stove, she set the copper teakettle on the burner and turned on the stove. Pausing a minute to rub at the ache in the back of her neck, she then turned toward the cupboard and reached up for a box of Earl Grey tea.

Jack watched her. He'd been sitting in the dark, thinking, when she'd come in. She looked very vulnerable just now, her feet bare, the hem of her gown dusting her ankles, the ruffle at her neck disappearing beneath her flowing hair. He wondered what it would be like to have her curl up beside him in his bed.

"Kids are all asleep."

She jumped. "Jack! Why didn't you make your presence known?"

He grinned. "I just did. I thought you were making it an early night. You seemed pretty upset with the kids. Can't sleep?"

She held on to the countertop and took a long, slow, deep breath before turning around to face him. "I haven't tried to sleep yet, if it's any of your business. I'm having some tea. I'll have it in my room."

"Tense, aren't we? Still blaming me for the broken lamp?"

Abby took a mug from the cupboard and set it loudly on the counter. "I'm not tense." She shot the words out too quickly. She was fast to cover them. "I'm a little miffed that the guy didn't call about the shop."

"Maybe something came up and he got stuck somewhere...."

She added two heaping spoonfuls of sugar to the cup. "Possible. Or maybe he has bad news and doesn't want to tell me."

"Do you always look for the worst-case scenario or are you just doing it this once?" he teased.

She shook her head. "It's just that I'm so anxious. Not only do I need to build this as a business for the boys, but I need it for a diversion for me. My mind, my brain, needs something new and different and separate from my old life to deal with. Do you understand that?"

"Was your old life so bad?"

"Not the part you see. I mean my life with Jim. What happened after his accident. Finding out about his mistress...and all the others. It seemed everyone at the office knew Jim was a womanizer. Just his silly little obedient wife never even suspected. I must have been a laughingstock for years. And when I think back on the excuses he gave me, on how gullible I was. I'll never put myself in that position again. No one will ever be able to fool me, 'cause I'll never care about another man for the rest of my life."

"Whew."

She had to laugh at her own tirade. "You started it."

"And all I set out to do was offer you my help

with your business. I can build just about anything you want.''

"I'll accept that. I want the front to have a new look also. And a name. I haven't come up with a name. I'm getting ahead of myself again.''

"It looks pretty on you. You're all flustered and your eyes are lit up.''

He was just paying her an offhand compliment. She should stop being so suspicious of every move he made. She wanted to accept it graciously and move on. She couldn't.

She looked at him. "This is one of the things I hadn't thought about, Jack. My lack of privacy. I'm used to having the entire house to myself at any hour of the day or night.''

"Are you telling me to mind my own business or that I should stay cooped up in my room as soon as the kids are tucked in for the night?''

"That does seem a bit ridiculous, doesn't it?''

He simply looked at her. In another house, he might have found the seclusion welcome. Like the situation he'd left several months ago. Isolation was better than sharing space with his ex-wife. But here he found himself looking forward to spending time with Abby. He liked watching the way every thought and emotion worked its way across her features.

"Just because I have a hard time trusting the male species in any circumstance isn't your fault,'' she admitted, then leaned back against the counter to wait for the water to boil.

"Never mind. I've been meaning to talk to you about the boys' summer camp. It's only a four-hour-a-day thing. Starts soon. I marked the day on the calendar. They went last year and liked it. Lanyards.

Remember them? Yellow, red, blue. All colors. I must have braided everyone in my family a necklace and a key chain. And they used them, too, bless them, until I forgot about it.''

''We carved stuff. Bears that looked like round blobs with round knobs. Rabbits that resembled eggs with tails. My childhood was pretty simple compared to today. Even with the divorce and everything. My parents didn't fight over me or use me against one another. They wanted me to have contact. What happened to all those uncomplicated days?''

''Don't know. I had a great time when I was a kid. I went from neighbor house to neighbor house without worry. My parents didn't know exactly where I was for hours at a time. I wouldn't think of that now.''

She fixed her tea and took it to the table, where he was sitting in the shadows.

''Can I get you something else?''

''Abby, I live here now, remember? If I want something, I'll get it, but thank you anyway. I don't want you to feel you have to wait on me.''

''No. I won't. You, either.''

A quiet, comfortable moment passed between them.

She voiced her thoughts out loud. ''Why were you sitting here in the dark?''

''Unwinding. Planning. Thinking what is the best way to get my business back on track.''

''Not the kids, huh?''

''Nope. Kids are kids. It'll all work out. You're making it harder than it has to be. You don't have to spend your entire life thinking about the kids. They're sleeping for now. Let your mind relax.''

A little insulted, she sipped her tea and tilted her head to one side. "I see, divorced Dr. Murdock. And where did you get your degree in human relations?"

"Same place you got yours, I suspect."

"Touché. So now you see, very clearly, why I feel I need a live-in male to help me with the kids. I'm losing the ability to make levelheaded decisions, to even see things with the right perspective anymore."

"You just have too many things going on at once. And I think you're taking raising those boys way too seriously. Kids have a way of raising themselves. They just need a guiding hand on their shoulder. I practically raised myself and I didn't turn out all bad. I spent most of my days out hunting or fishing. School was just a thing you had to get through to find your way back to the tree house. I was inside only when I had to be. My parents sat back, stopped me when I was on the wrong course, encouraged me when I was on the right course and bingo! Here I am."

"I guess sniping at each other won't help any of us. I'm so used to having to be absolutely correct, perfectly on the mark every minute. When you're the only one with the responsibility..."

"So let up now. You're not the only one here with responsibility. Relax."

"Easier said than done." Her voice sounded sleepy even to her.

"Not really."

"I'm still dealing." She ran an impatient hand through her hair.

He crossed his arms and sat back in the chair. "Okay. With what, exactly?"

She shrugged. "Stuff."

He waited a beat to see if she would elaborate on

her own. When she didn't, he tried to control the irritation in his voice. He shouldn't berate someone about carrying old baggage around with them. "That stuff with Jim is over and done with now. He can't hurt you anymore."

She took a deep breath and said the words out loud. That wasn't nearly as hard as coming to the realization that she needed to talk to someone about it. "So, magician, tell me how to rid myself of all this built-up bitterness."

Disgust was now quite evident in Jack's voice. "Don't limit yourself. All men aren't alike."

It was nice that the news that Jim was a womanizer angered Jack. That told her another good thing about him.

He lifted his eyes from his coffee and pinned her directly. "I knew there had to be more to your hang-ups than your relationship with the kids. You have a chip on your shoulder the size of Texas. A way of looking at the world through distrustful eyes. So, I'm here now. Talk to me."

It annoyed her that she felt she needed to dump on him. She forced a smile as she met his gaze. "I told you I didn't find out about his affairs until after his death. I was that stupid."

"Or maybe he was that clever."

"Thanks, but I had to be really dumb not to realize there was something going on." She shook her head. "Maybe I closed my eyes to it. Could I have done that?"

"Probably, but I think you're too smart for that. Some men can successfully lead two separate lives and no one ever knows."

"Everywhere I go, everyone I see. I feel that they

know and are laughing at me. I'm hoping this flower shop will keep me so busy and introduce me to so many new people that all those days of humiliation will be behind me. If it doesn't...well, I'm afraid I'm really going to lose it one of these days.''

"Have you ever considered moving away? If it bothers you that much, it might be the answer.''

"Of course, but it would just be another upset for the boys. Their school and friends are here. And I guess to me, it would be the coward's way out.''

"So you're pretty mixed-up right now.''

She laughed. "I guess that sums it up pretty good.''

"We can be a help to each other.'' He reached over and ran his hand across her shoulder. His touch was hotter than the tea she sipped. "I'm a little starved for attention and conversation myself. You can only discuss so much with a two-year-old.''

Abby's arm noodled from his touch as she raised the cup to her lips. The liquid soothed and warmed as it made its way to her stomach.

She set the cup down and wiggled from under his touch. "I can't do much for you.''

"You already are. This new home atmosphere, being around you and the boys. It's not only good for Katie. It's good for me.''

Jack moved to the sink and put his coffee cup down, then walked back to the table. He stood behind her, not touching her. His hands remained at his sides. At this moment, this very moment, he wanted her. He knew it was simply male-female attraction. Hormones. He knew it wasn't ever going to happen. He wouldn't let it. He might start to care too much. And that certainly couldn't happen again. Jack Murdock was a fool over a woman only once.

He had to leave the room. "Good night."

"Good night, Jack. And thanks."

She sat for a while, after Jack had gone up, in the dimly lit kitchen. Her mind was spinning with ideas and excitement. Now she would probably never get to sleep. Turning out the light, she headed for her room.

On her way, she heard a noise in Katie's bedroom. Abby turned to check on her. Katie had been fighting a cold and she wanted to be sure she wasn't getting sicker. Abby turned the doorknob and opened the door just a crack.

Katie was up but she wasn't alone or sick. Her daddy was there, wearing only green-and-white-striped pajama bottoms, his hair glistening wet from a shower. A light from the bedside giraffe lamp cast the room in a soft golden glow. Jack appeared the pirate with his dark five-o'clock shadow and wide shoulders. His stomach flat. His feet bare.

Katie's little ballerina music box that sat on her dresser was playing, the pink figurine leaping and spinning in the semidarkness. Katie's feet were on top of her daddy's. Her hands were raised over her head and held in his. Jack danced gently and easily as he stumbled along with the tune, not knowing all the words. Their shadows loomed huge against the walls. Katie's head fell back, and her beautiful childish laughter tumbled into the room.

What love. What devotion. What dedication. Abby felt happiness for Katie and sadness for herself. She missed being loved so. She missed the unconditional love she knew existed between so many people in so many different relationships.

"More, Daddy, more."

Jack turned slow circles, and dipped and swayed.

Abby moved to pull the door shut when Katie saw her and squealed her name. Caught! She pushed the door all the way open.

"Sorry, Jack. I heard noises and I thought her cold might be... I'm sorry for interrupting. Go night-night, Katie. I'll see you in the morning."

Katie wailed and held her hand out for Abby to join them.

She garbled something in two-year-old talk that translated to "Go ring-around-the-rosy with Katie."

Totally embarrassed, especially under Jack's smug grin, Abby came closer and joined hands with them. They bobbed and circled and hummed to the tune. After a bit, Katie yawned and her eyelids began to close. Abby was relieved. She pulled her fingers from Jack's hand and picked up the sleepy child.

"Give Daddy a kiss. It's time for bed." Abby held Katie up so she could give Daddy a juicy smack on the cheek. Jack encircled both of them in a big bear hug. Abby held her breath as he proceeded to kiss them both on the cheek.

His rough jaw scraped at her face. His mouth, though the touch was fleeting, had been warm and firm. This was too intimate. Much too familiar. But it had happened so innocently. So spontaneously. To make anything of it would be to draw attention to the vibes echoing through her torso.

Abby shooed Jack from the room and laid the little girl down in her bed. Within minutes the child was asleep. Taking this unmeasured moment, Abby sat in the rocker that was close to Katie's bed and just watched her. What would she do when Katie left? How would she react when Jack left and took this beautiful little girl with him? Later, she'd think of that later. She could deal with anything. Hadn't she already dealt with the worst?

Abby bustled out into the hallway. Jack was waiting there for her, leaning against the wall, arms folded, feet crossed at the ankles.

His voice was lazy and sleepy. "For a minute there, I almost thought we were a real family instead of just stand-ins for each other."

"Good night, Jack." She made a move to walk past him.

His voice was low, and she barely heard his "Thank you."

She stopped and turned back to him. "For what?"

"I know we're not really a family here. That you and I aren't really married and raising these kids. That this is all temporary. You're not really my wife, Ben and Nick aren't really my kids. But it's all so nice. So damn nice that it's hard to believe it's pretend."

She was flattered and moved by his words. Too much so. The feel of his lips on her face was still too fresh in her mind. Her stomach was still in a knot.

She turned to go before more was said. The hall was dark and quiet, and a lean-on-him feeling was coming over her again. Much stronger this time.

He didn't move as she swept past him and into her room. He heard her shut the door gently and move away from it. Good thing. He'd been caught up in the tender moment, and if she had stayed, he would've made a fool of himself and kissed her.

Chapter Six

A long week of negotiations finally paid off. It was worth every worrisome minute, every nail-biting decision. Mr. Morrison knew what he wanted and he wanted cash. Abby needed to be sure she had working capital. She also wanted to be sure she was paying a reasonable price, so she spent a good amount of time going over his hand-kept accounting books. She made projections, she speculated, she prayed. And made her final offer.

It was her first and maybe only major decision made on her own. Jim had always been the one to plan things and follow through on them. She never lacked anything, but perhaps he'd never given her the opportunity to find out what she wanted. She knew that now but not then.

The good news about the flower shop came by telephone just before lunch. Abby nearly jumped up from behind her desk and shouted it to the world, but she knew no one there would care. She reined in her exuberance. She had to finish the day and then at home, during dinner, she would make the announcement.

She stopped short. The heck with that. Minutes ago she was a temp. But now she was a shop owner! She gathered her things, mumbled some excuse to the boss and left.

Freedom! She felt suddenly untethered, floating three feet above the ground. Bouncing out into the bright sunshine and the balmy breeze, she had the urge to jump down the steps and bellow to the people walking by. *Here comes Abigail Roberts. Entrepreneur! Look out, world!*

The boys had no idea about this. She hadn't wanted to share it with them until it was definite. And now it was. She didn't really expect them to realize the value of the news at their age, but she was certainly hoping for cooperation.

Her offer had been accepted, and they could sign the papers and exchange the money that Friday afternoon. In four days. So quickly! It seemed that Mr. Morrison was in a hurry to begin his retirement. She was just as anxious to start her stint as shop owner. By Saturday morning, the place would be hers. She couldn't wait to see the look on Jack's face.

Jack. She realized she couldn't wait to tell him! And that didn't seem as odd as it should.

Jack had been very happy for her and supportive the times they discussed all the possibilities. His offer to help her appeared genuine. He seemed eager to work by her side on this new project. This was foreign to her. Completely novel.

Weird, she thought as she jumped in her car and started it. Everything had changed so quickly when she'd thought it couldn't change at all. Was it just the addition of Jack to their lives or was it a combination of her new resolve to move forward? It had to be Jack. His presence. His promise of help. The fact that when he looked at her, she felt she could accomplish anything.

She couldn't resist. Instead of driving straight home, she stopped at the flower shop, pretended to be a browsing customer while she took another look around. Ideas whirled around in her mind. Changes, additions, deletions. Holidays would be wonderful fun. The boys could learn to be a big help. It would truly be a family business.

Mr. Morrison wasn't to be found, so she simply introduced herself to the clerk behind the counter and took her time. It was almost like having another child. Looking at it, imagining what it would turn out to be. The shop needed grooming, coaxing, loving care.

Hers. All hers. And the boys'. She would encourage them to input ideas. She would incorporate some of them and let them learn the feeling of accomplishment. They liked growing things, and she would section off a place in the work shed out back for each of them. She would teach them to deal with the customers. Especially Nick, who was old enough. Oh, this was going to be a wonderful adventure. She felt like Alice looking down the rabbit hole.

She paused by a container of daisies and then on impulse pulled out a handful. They were soft and velvety as she brushed them across her face. Abby marched to the cashier.

One clothespin in his mouth while he curled a collar over the line, Jack let his mind wander. This wasn't at all how he had it planned. It was all sup-

posed to take much longer. He'd never thought it
would go so smoothly. He'd never dared to think that
the addition of one lovely woman and her two blond-
haired boys would make such a difference in his life.
He felt good. Every morning, waking up was a pleasure instead of a chore. Katie had been the one shining star in his life. Now he had an entire constellation.

Katie was taking a nap. The boys were down the
road with the Jamison kids building a tree house.
He'd just finished talking to Dallas, his foreman,
about the Townsend job they had bid for and won.
They would break ground on the first new project as
soon as the permits and inspections began. Things
were going so well, it was spooky.

But he'd kept one promise to himself: distance.
More emotional than physical. And he was proud of
himself that he was able to keep that resolution even
when he found himself, more and more, thinking
about Abby. In more and more ways. He pushed the
thoughts from his head, reminding himself he was
simply a healthy male with a healthy male's appetites.

He was concentrating on hanging the clothes when
he heard Abby's car come up the driveway.

Seeing Jack engaging in such an ordinary task
pierced her heart. His hands were too big for the
clothespins. He towered over the umbrella-type
clothesline. The shirts were hung by the collars instead of the tails. The baby clothes were hung with
one pin instead of two. And the picture of him, tall
and lean in snug blue jeans, swinging around, tripping
over the clothes basket to greet her with a huge grin
on his face, the breeze ruffling his hair, nearly burst
her heart.

For the first time, the very first time, she allowed

herself to acknowledge she was happy. And it wasn't just the flower shop. It very much had to do with the addition of Jack Murdock to her life. As a companion, a helper, she reminded herself quickly. Nothing else. Never anything else.

She jumped from the car and walked swiftly to where he was working.

"You're home early."

"Yep." She marched right up to him and held out her hand filled with the daisies.

He looked at them and back to her glowing face. It could only mean one thing. "You got your flower shop."

Grinning wide, she nodded her head. Eyes sparkling, body nearly jumping out of her clothes, she shouted, "I got my flower shop!"

Without thinking, he picked her up and pulled her to him and wheeled her around in a big circle, two or three times. "That's great news. We have to celebrate. We'll take the kids out to dinner tonight and a movie." He kissed her cheek soundly, then put her feet back on the ground only to grab her arms once again as she swayed to catch her balance.

Certainly it wasn't the hard, full-length contact of her body with his that made her dizzy. It couldn't possibly be the strong, confident arms that held her tightly against him if only for a moment. No way was it the fact that just being this close to him had her blood pounding through her veins. She wanted more contact. Her body screamed out for it.

No, no. It was only his exuberant greeting and that swing, her feet flying off the ground, that had winded her. There was nothing else between them.

Still holding the daisies in her hand, Abby extended

them toward him. "We'll call to have pizza delivered instead. I want to sit at the kitchen table and draw some more plans. Here, these are for you."

Never in his life had anyone given him flowers. Or even made such a thoughtful gesture. He was stunned. He didn't know how to accept them. What to do with them.

Seeing his confused look, Abby jumped in to explain her impulsive purchase before he could possibly read more into it than was intended. Just what had she intended? She shook her head. "They're a thank-you ahead of time for all the help you're going to give me. But I insist on paying you as I would anyone who did the carpentry work."

Head cocked to the side, one hand stuffed in his pocket, he nodded curtly. "Then we're going to have a fight."

Dancing around, Abby bounced. "Not today, we're not. I can't believe this is really happening. Friday I sign the papers. Saturday it's mine." She closed her hands over her heart. "I don't want to close down even for a day, so it's going to be a real mess at first. You'll have to put in some long hours with the kids."

"That's my job. Let me fix you a glass of lemonade, Ms. Flower Shop Owner. I'm glad for you, Abby. I like seeing you happy." They walked into the house arm in arm, leaving the remaining clothes in the basket to be hung later.

Later that night, Jack and Abby sat at the kitchen table with pencils and paper for the better part of the evening.

"What's the big deal anyway?" Ben asked Nick

as they sat in front of the television watching a favorite movie, overloaded with cola and pizza.

Nick didn't take his eyes off the television screen. "Mom's happy, dumbo. That's what's the big deal."

"A flower store is dumb. It's just for girls."

"Is not. You just don't like anything anymore, Benny. Ever since Dad died, you've been mad."

"Have not!"

"Have to! That's why you don't like Jack. And that's dumb, too. He's a nice guy and he likes you."

Abby stopped the motion of Jack's pencil on paper and shushed his talking so she could hear what was being said by the kids.

"He just needed a mom for Katie. He doesn't like us. It's his job."

She watched hurt flit across Jack's eyes before it was willed to disappear. She touched his hand.

"Well, he likes me. Now be quiet and watch television."

She shook her head. "I told you it wouldn't be easy."

"He needs more time. Don't let it get to you. Now," Jack said, redirecting his thoughts to the sketches on the table, "what about this wall?"

Abby sat back in the chair and sighed. "I appreciate this."

"What?"

"Your taking time to help me decide how to fix the place up. Your enthusiasm."

"How can a man deny anything that puts that kind of light in your eyes?" She was beautiful, and he was hard put to simply enjoy it and not dwell on it. He didn't want a woman that way. Friends. That's all it would be. All it could be. He'd promised himself he'd always keep part of himself for himself. No one would ever be able to touch his heart.

A warm wash of pleasure floated over her. She couldn't pull her gaze from him. There was such life there, such an offering of...of what?

And there it was again. That feeling of being liked. Accepted. He was genuinely pleased for her. Genuinely interested and seemed to have no doubt at all that she could make a go of it. Jim would have questioned her ability right off, made her doubt herself.

Trust. It had sneaked up on her, but here she was trusting again when she thought she never would. She had to, actually. She had to depend on Jack's offer of help, his good judgment where the kids were concerned. It had drifted over into her own life, as well.

"You're not going to try to run this thing all by yourself, are you?"

"Of course not. I'm the boss. I already talked to the three girls that work there, and they were happy I offered them their jobs."

"Good, because you promised the kids the carnival Saturday night."

"Ohh," she sighed. "I was planning on spending the entire day at the shop. It's the first day and all."

"You'll have hundreds of days. You only have so many promises. Besides, you'll probably wear yourself out before supper. You'll be relieved to just sit on some giant swooping, swinging metal ride and have the hell scared out of you."

She'd dreamed it up, she told herself as she rose to get one more piece of pizza; that line of sparks that seemed to strongly connect the two of them for a brief moment. Her life was going to be complicated enough starting the new business without having to deal with a runaway imagination.

"I seriously doubt that, but you're right. We have to go. Anyway, first thing Saturday morning, let's get the kids up early, take them to breakfast and get to the shop. I'll show the boys the greenhouse and let them choose where they want their little spot. Do you want a spot to grow things, Jack?"

"Me with delicate petals and tiny pots and even tinier seeds and…ribbons and bows? I'll pass."

"Well, I didn't know. I thought I'd ask."

"You're bubbling again."

"Tough. Now, about the new sign for over the door. Can you paint the letters in the old-fashioned style and with the smaller letters Proprietor Abby Roberts over here near the corner?"

"Not 'Abigail'?"

"No. Abigail was the other me. From now on, I'll be known to everyone as Abby. It has a friendlier sound to it. Don't you think?"

"I like it."

Relaxing back in her chair, she found herself looking back and surprised at not feeling like hiding. Not jumping to condemn herself for being stupid. "Moving forward is enabling me to think back, go over my life with Jim without nearly as much bitterness. It's happening. The very thing I thought never would. Before you came along, I couldn't change my perspective. I was sort of stuck, treading water, not sure which way to turn. Almost immediately after you moved in, I felt free to try things because there was someone else around to help if I failed. I'm beginning to feel invincible. It only comes in spurts and jumps, but soon it'll be the way I feel all the time, I hope."

"That's as it should be, Abby."

She laughed softly. "What about you? Have you managed to dump the baggage from your other life?"

Jack bounced the pencil against the palm of his hand. "It's sliding off. You and the boys have proved to me that I couldn't have been solely responsible for the failure of that marriage. Granted, we haven't been housemates for a long time, but we all get along very well, and it just keeps getting better."

"We're a pair. And we do work well together. Synchronized."

He was too close, he realized as he watched her bend her head forward over their sketches. He was too close to stepping over the line he had drawn for himself a year ago. He'd told himself to never think about having a wife again. To depend only on himself for whatever he needed. To never ever put himself in a position to be stepped on. To never hang his feelings out to be laughed at. To never, never let any woman touch his heart again. But Abby made it so easy to ignore all those promises. And the word *partners* kept running through his mind. And it didn't have anything to do with her new business.

She looked up just then, and caught a different look in his eyes. Just what that expression was she couldn't define, but it left her feeling good. She wanted nothing more than to lean forward and rest her mouth on his. If they were married, if they were a real family, she would do just that. And more.

Her insides were burning. She attributed it to mere excitement about the shop. But down, deep down, in that little-known corner of her heart, she knew that it was him. That man. The one sitting across the table from her drawing straight lines with a No. 2 pencil.

He alone had given her that little bit of courage and hope to move forward. And she would never forget that even if she could never do anything about it.

Saturday morning found the Roberts and Murdock families running helter-skelter around the grounds of the new business. The boys' interest piqued as soon as they were turned loose in the greenhouse. Katie toddled around tipping over flowerpots and falling over coils of hose.

Abby was like a whirlwind of energy. Excitement shone from her eyes, quivered in her voice, and just watching it was a new experience for Jack. She was like a first-time racehorse filled with excitement and fear waiting at the starting gate for the gun to go off. Her exhilaration was his. Her energy conveyed itself to him. He liked seeing her so animated and hopeful. He liked seeing her, period.

Jack and Abby went from one spot to another stretching the measuring tape from one corner to the next and standing back to plan. She shifted this display to that shelf and that display to the window. Abby handled nearly every exhibit, commenting on how cute the ceramic vase was or how quaint the little basket was. As customers came and went, Abby made sure she spoke to them and offered her help.

"You're going to be good at this. The customers appreciate your extra personal touch."

It was then she realized. "Good heavens, Jack." She tiptoed up close to his ear and whispered, "I don't know any of the technical stuff I'm supposed to know."

He laughed then, good and hearty. Throwing his arm around her shoulder, he shook a little confidence into her. "You know the difference between a rose and a tulip, don't you? How hard can it be? You bunch all the different colors together and tie it with a ribbon."

He was being ridiculous, but she had scared herself to the point of not listening to his ramblings.

"Yes, but—" she rolled out of his embrace and turned in a circle, her arms held out in front of her "—I don't know about fertilizer and water...which plants get a lot and which get a little? Good grief, I jumped into something I know absolutely nothing about."

He pushed her toward the back room. "That's not all so bad. It's not even a problem. Learning is interesting. Experimenting is fun. Uncovering a new piece of information is like being an explorer. Each discovery is better than the last."

He wasn't talking about horticulture at this point, but he kept that thought to himself. He wanted to lift that thick curl that lay against her shoulder. He was simply bewitched by this lady.

No, he mentally talked back to the voice in his head. He was under control. He was a man with a resolution and he would keep it. Enjoying her meant nothing serious.

"The library. I'll begin there and then I'll subscribe to some magazines." She made notes on a shorthand pad. "Build my own library. Maybe I'll check with the junior college. They might have some courses I should take."

Jack leaned back against the wall and just watched. He felt peaceful in the face of a tornado.

She stopped suddenly. "Oh, Jack, do you think I've made a big mistake?"

He shook his head. "Other than hiring me to be the kids' nanny, you probably just made the wisest decision of your life. The girls out front ought to know something. Just ask them for their help."

He was so logical. Big problems became dwarfed as he dealt with them. He paved the way and made life so much easier. She deeply appreciated that he so effortlessly gave her what she needed. The effort was in forcing herself to remember...to think of him as a friend. Nothing else.

"You know," she commented as she walked over and patted him on the shoulder, "you make everything seem so simple. Without more than just being here, you clear things up. Hard stuff seems simple. Things that might scare me don't seem so hair-raising just now. How do you do that?"

"Can't say I do it for everyone. Some people you ask might tell you I make life very, very difficult."

"Then they'd be wrong. Thanks, Jack. I owe you."

"In fact, my ex-wife would tell you I'm insensitive, boorish and uncouth. She said I ruined her life."

Abby shook her head as she went around to the far side of the potting table and began to pull on it. "You could, I guess, if you set out to, but I sincerely doubt she ever really knew you. I sure don't see that side of you."

He got on the other end of the table. "Where are you going with this?"

"Closer to the door. I have to be able to watch the kids while I work."

"Don't try to struggle with it yourself. I'm here."

She didn't look up at him. Couldn't. He was being so damn nice and trying to be so helpful that she wanted to hug him.

With his help, the table slid easily the few feet to the doorway. Abby heard the crack as they settled the table and watched as Jack bent over.

"Leg's splitting. I'll be back."

Abby watched as he walked out to his truck and yanked a huge, heavy toolbox from the bed. She liked watching him move. Muscles bunched and relaxed. He swaggered instead of walked. He was confident. There was an aura of power about him that made people notice him right away.

Now, hammer in hand, he repaired the table with the help of a few well-placed nails.

Nick and Ben appeared, Katie in tow. There was mud on the knees of her overalls. The yellow ribbons Abby had pinned in her hair were gone and there was a ring of dirt around her mouth.

Nick cast a very grown-up look Jack's way. "Don't worry, Jack, it's just plain old dirt."

Chapter Seven

Carnival! Just the sound of those specific syllables caused the boys to jiggle up and down and Katie to clap her hands. Even Abby succumbed to the stimulation, the remembrance of what it was to be a child. The anticipation. The thrill.

They spotted the tallest of the rides psychedelically striking out into the sky, then field after field of parked cars and trucks. And then they heard it: music, the calliope, the clarinet, the strains of "Little Eva" climbing into the air.

Magic. The rhythm of the barker's voice. "Come one, come all, and see tonight what you've never seen before. The bearded lady. A man who swallows swords. The fire-eater. Step inside the big top. Watch the dancing ponies, clap for the acrobatic dogs, and the lions, the most ferocious beasts of all...watch as Jamal the Lion Tamer puts his head in Sebastian's mouth."

Children laughing. Parents shouting. Target rifles

firing at metal ducks. Pennies sliding across glass dishes. Baseballs thudding into canvas. Balloons popping.

Machinery. The whir of the Tilt-a-Whirl. The clack of the roller coaster as it climbed toward the night sky. The loud sway of the pirate ship as it swung like a pendulum, back, hold...and forth, pitching everyone downward into a powerful swing upward and almost upside down...hold...pause...hover and swoop...down again among the squeals of the daredevils and the screams of the fainthearted.

The air. Driving. Twirling. Electric. Charged with excitement and anticipation. The current wound its way down the fairway, cascaded down the Octopus and hooped around the Ferris wheel, curling free and running loose to find another path to follow.

Neon lights, red, yellow, green. Balloons, orange, blue, pink.

Now that darkness had descended and added its own depth of excitement to the fairway, the crowd increased. Families. Strollers. Couples holding hands. Older folks, remembering. Single guys on the lookout for a new babe. Beautiful young girls, heads together, giggling and pointing to a tall, gangly young man.

Ben was beside himself with enthusiasm. This time last year, no one had been in the mood to attend, so little Ben could hardly remember the last time he'd been here. His feet spent very little time on the ground.

He had a death grip on his mother's hand as he pulled her along. "Hurry, Mom, look at that. Oh, look!" he shouted. "Look over there! Elephants."

"Whoa there, cowboy." Jack ruffled Ben's hair. Katie was sitting on Jack's shoulders. She held on by putting two tiny hands across his forehead. He anchored her by holding her feet. "We'll get to it all."

Ben smoothed his hair back down and turned away from Jack. Ben still wouldn't give in to Jack. And they had come so close so many times.

"Can we ride the Ferris wheel first, can we, huh?" He directed his question toward Abby.

Nick piped up as he jumped circles around Ben, "I'm doing the haunted house first. If you're coming with me, you have to do it now."

"We're all sticking together," Abby directed. "No one strikes out on their own if we happen to turn our backs or something. Do you hear that?"

Two male heads bobbed up and down, but before that thought could be completely absorbed, they were running ahead, though staying close, toward the silly-looking house with scary faces painted all over it.

Jack peeled off. "I'll go get loaded up with tickets."

Abby watched Jack become enfolded in the crowd and then saunter back with practically an entire roll of red tickets. How could just the sight of him please her more than she could explain?

They began the rounds with the haunted house.

As they approached the line for the terror trip, Ben spotted a little brown puppy romping toward the back of the building.

"Hey, Mom, look! A dog. I'll bet he's lost. I'll go get him." He took off at a run.

"Come back here right this minute. You leave that puppy alone. He probably belongs to someone close by and he just got loose. You stay here."

"Aw, Mom, he might be scared." Ben dropped his arms to his sides. "It's noisy here. And getting dark."

"You don't know anything about that dog. It could be sick." Abby used her warning-mother voice.

Ben crossed his arms over his chest and looked at the ground. A stance that Jack had grown used to seeing.

Abby eyed the crooked, mirror-lined doorway and looked down at her son. "Ben, are you sure you want to go in there? It looks like it's for older boys."

"Of course he is." Jack gave Ben a little shove to go on with Nick. "Nothing like having the stuffing scared out of you." The two boys bounded toward the line.

Abby reacted swiftly. "If I didn't want him to go in there, he shouldn't have."

"Lighten up, Abby. I am their nanny," he teased. "That does give me certain space to direct them."

"Maybe he's a little too young for all that...gore or whatever's in there."

"And maybe you need to let go of him a little."

She kept her mouth shut as they looked around and waited for the two boys to come out so they could move on. She had to remind herself that she had hired Jack to do exactly this job, and he was simply doing it. Still, she just wasn't used to it.

A few minutes later, they ran out. Whooping and hollering at the top of their lungs, each describing a different abhorrence to a different person.

Ben had a pride shining in his eyes. His voice was filled with awe. "And the coffin opened up and there was a real live mummy in it and he reached out and grabbed my arm right here!"

Abby stood back and watched with amazement as Ben spun his tale breathlessly, directing his words to Jack.

Jack squatted down and tested Ben's arm. "Right here?"

"Yep, right there. I'll bet I have a bruise tomorrow."

Jack laughed and ruffled the boy's hair. This time Ben didn't make his automatic move to smooth it back into place. He bounced on to catch up to Nick.

"A miniature breakthrough," Jack gloated, and winked down at Abby, who pretended to ignore him.

The little sports-car ride that merely went in circles was next in line.

"This is a baby ride," Ben objected.

"It sure is." Jack answered him. "And you're going to go with Katie."

"Okay. But I won't like it."

Abby stood back and watched as Jack loaded Katie and Ben into the little car, saw that they were safely belted in and gave a list of instructions of his own. Her thoughts took her tired brain captive and proceeded their own way. If only this were real. How simple life would be. Jack taking care of her, his wife, and the kids, his kids.

A shiver rode through her, and reality came with it. She wanted none of those things. She had been there, done that. Thought it was all so great and it hadn't been.

They ate pink cotton candy, foot-long hot dogs and fat, greasy fries from a paper cone. Jack won a doll for Katie by pinging twelve ducks in a row. Abby won an orange ostrich for popping five balloons with five darts. She walked the carnival grounds with the stuffed animal slung over her shoulder.

The Tilt-a-Whirl loomed before them, with its half-moon-shaped cars that rotated fiercely in place and at the same time spun around on a vast moving and gyrating floor.

"When I was a kid, you couldn't get me off those things." Abby laughed and shook her head.

Before she knew what was happening Jack took Abby by the hand, pushed the boys ahead of him and grabbed tons of red tickets from the roll jammed in his pocket.

"No! Oh, no...I said when I was younger, I loved this ride. I don't want to ride it now. It's been so many years. And Katie's too little for this."

Jack completely ignored Abby's protests, and the boys galloped along, laughing and excited to see their mom on the ride. They made their way to one of the cars. Jack took the seat on the outside, while Abby held back and let the boys get in the car before she did.

"You're going to squish the kids if you don't move over here next to me," Jack warned, grinning.

"Yeah, that's right, Mom, let us squish you this time."

After a moment's hesitation, she relented, remembering that the last person in was usually the one pushed hardest against the rest of them by gravity. She kept Nick next to her and let Ben, the lightweight, sit on the outside.

The ride master walked by, took tickets, and lowered the curved bar locking them all in. There was no turning back now. The thrill of anticipation rippled through her body. Jack raised his arm and lowered it over her shoulder. The simple titillation of male against female trembled through her entire being. They sat that way waiting as the ride master made his

way to all the other cars, collecting tickets and se-
curing the passengers.

"You might be sorry you pushed this," she
warned.

"Ms. Roberts, anything that gets you this close to
me won't make me sorry."

The hidden meaning to his words speared through
her. He was flirting again without even realizing it.
He was so used to joking and clowning around, how
was she supposed to know when to take him seriously? She knew this wasn't one of those times. Was
it?

She wanted to move Jack's arm but couldn't see
the sense in even validating that it was there. It was
only to make enough room in the car for all of them
to sit comfortably. That her body was reacting was
simply her fault. She was grown-up. She was in control. Lordy, she wanted him to tighten his grip. Pull
her closer.

The ride lurched forward.

The music picked up in tempo. Nick raised his
arms high, defying fear. Ben followed suit. Abby
grabbed the bar tightly, cramping her fingers on the
cold steel. Jack relaxed, a grin on his face, one huge
protective arm now around his daughter.

The ride increased in speed. The car tilted and
whirled on its own circular track. First slowly and
then very fast, hanging on the top tilt a second or two
before swaying down and around and around. Now
all the cars on the one huge, spiraling, twisting and
twirling platform leapt up and down and around and
around at the same time but in different directions.

Force shoved Ben against Nick. Ben and Nick were

being pasted against their mom. Abby, Ben and Nick flattened against Jack.

Abby ended up full-out pressed against Jack from head to foot. Her head was compressed against his chest. She could feel his laughter rumble beneath her ear. He was hard and sturdy, and she knew nothing could hurt her as long as he was between her and the danger. Sometimes she felt compelled to throw good sense to the wind, toss what she knew was good for her out the window. It would be so nice to just go with her heart instead of her head.

The boys squealed as the car lurched the other way, momentarily separating all four occupants of the car. Two seconds passed before the car spun wildly again, the platform tilting almost straight up and down. All three slid back into Jack and Katie one more time.

Blood that already raced through her veins from the excitement of the ride, now tore through her at breakneck speed. Her pulse tripped heavily, and her heart pounded. Butterflies tornadoed in her stomach, fanning the heat that built inside her.

Her cotton shorts and bare legs rubbed against his jeans. Her bare arm and thin cotton shirt caressed his denim-covered chest. Just then, he tightened the arm he had around her shoulder, his fingers twining with hers when she grabbed for his hand to hold on.

Fire leapt. Flames licked. The world was a blur. The ride whirled on, and at this moment she wished it would never stop. Reality was nowhere. Nowhere was everywhere.

In her mind, despite the turmoil of the ride, she could picture the car coming loose from the track, only she and Jack aboard. It hurtled out toward space like something in a cartoon. Jack's mouth was on hers as he laid her back in the seat.

The boys' screams of happy terror and Katie's squeals brought her back to reality with a thud. She tried to push away from Jack, but it only heightened the sensitivity of being melded together.

She wanted to turn and raise her face to his, to taste his mouth and see what gravity could do to the joining of lips. She wanted him to fold her into his arms and keep the world away from her if just for a little while.

Suddenly it seemed the boys yahooed and screamed from miles away. Jack had stopped laughing and was pulling her closer to him. His lips were at her temple...the fingers of his other hand beneath her chin....

What a ride! Even if it was all only fantasy and only temporary, the exhilaration, the temptation, the thrill of it all, was good for her. She felt so alive, so animated! She felt ready to conquer the world. And she had a very strong urge to throw both her arms around this man and kiss him till he hollered uncle!

The ride slowed. The music kept beat. The cold night air rushed over her as the platform came to a rest and the car rocked back and forth. She straightened up and pushed some distance between herself and Jack. New feelings, exotic feelings that were totally inexplicable, were washing over her like rain down a mountainside. She was powerless to stop the feelings, but she could and must stop the contact.

The boys were shoving at the bar long before the ride master made his way to them. They were running and jumping across the platform. Abby needed help. Jack took her hand and guided her from the car.

Putting his arm around her, he asked, concerned, "Are you all right?"

"Yes, of course. I think the cotton candy just got wrapped around the foot-long hot dog. I'll be fine in a minute. You better pay attention to your baby. She looks a little red in the face."

"Abby..."

"I'm okay, Jack. Don't fuss."

The ground was still spinning beneath her feet. And it sure wasn't from the Tilt-a-Whirl.

Abby shook Jack's arm away. Danger. The word flashed in her head as brightly as any neon sign here. She was being caught up in the lights and the sounds and the devil-may-care attitude of the evening. In the sensation of being part of a family. In the remembrance of being a happy group.

As much as she could, for the rest of the night, Abby kept a good distance from Jack. When the baby rides came in line, Abby couldn't help but watch and admire the way Jack secured Katie in the little airplanes or adjusted her on the tiny carousel with Nick standing by to hold on to her.

A heat built inside of her no matter how hard she fought it. Just from being around him. Jack was all man. He was kind and gentle. He was rough and tough. He was silent. He was loud. He was every man.

Another, different yearning consumed her. She openly admitted to herself tonight that she wished Katie were her own. A daughter. To dress in frilly lace. To take to ballet lessons. To send her brothers along on her first date. To be the other female in the household. How could being in this atmosphere bring about such strong realizations? It wasn't the first time she'd seen all of them out and about in the community atmosphere...but it was the first time she'd seen how well they all fit together. That was all. It was really quite simple. She wished.

They had all fit together so well at the flower shop today. Working together. Joking around and being silly. Companionship was all she needed, she told herself. But her body craved more.

Was a relationship with Jack becoming something she wanted to see happen? Was it something she had to think about working toward? No. Not again. Could she ever put all her hopes, all her dreams and all her trust in the arms of a man? Absolutely not. Well, she didn't think so. Even one as good as Jack? No. Jim had seemed to be a good man, too. And in his way, she knew he had been. But it had all crumbled when she had faced reality. And there were other people involved in this equation. The boys. She couldn't ever risk hurting them again.

The big brightly lit carousel was next. Even Abby admitted she had to go for this one. It brought back too many childhood memories for her to pass it by.

Abby knew which animal was hers right away. The big colorful horse on the outside, his molded mane flying upward, his strong legs frozen in full gallop. One that went up and down as the platform went around. The boys split and chose giraffes and tigers up farther.

Jack appeared and threw a leg over the horse beside Abby's, Katie wrapping her little fingers around the pole automatically.

"That one doesn't go up and down," she warned him.

"Around is plenty for me." He grinned at her. Her

face had taken on the wonder of a child. Her eyes
had captured the glee of riding the wind. Watching
her would be all the ride he needed.

It began slowly at first, the horses delicately pranc-
ing. Then, as the music picked up, the speed increased. The horses galloped after the lions and tigers
and bears. The audience was a blur. The cooling night
air picked up her hair and trailed it out behind her.
Gravity pressed her clothes tight against her. And lib-
erty tingled through her.

She held tightly to the brass pole and leaned back,
hair flying, face turned upward, laughing. She knew
that if she let go, she would fall. The momentum of
the ride would carry her off into the night to crash
against the ground. So the trick was not to let go.
Hold on. Hold on and ride for all it was worth.

Jack watched Abby. Life could be wonderful. It
could be good. It didn't have to be the way it had
been for him the past year or so. And it never would
be again if for no other reason than in a very unrea-
sonably short time he'd come to care about this family. They would always be in each other's lives no
matter what. The boys. Abby.

She saw him watching her, smiling and enjoying
the fact that she was having a ball. Without letting
herself think, she reached out a hand toward him and,
when he leaned sideways to take it, she felt special.
Surely it was the combination of the carnival atmosphere, the magic, the promise of good things yet to
come, but she wanted to feel this way. If only for a
little while.

And for that little while, Abby let herself go and
just felt and enjoyed. And made a wish...that she
could feel this way always. Yet as everything does,

the ride ended. But not her mood. She was happy and carefree, even if her stomach was rebelling.

Soon they all found themselves at the foot of the Ferris wheel. Abby groaned. "I think I'll pass."

"Come on, Mom. There's nothing to this one. All you have to do is sit and it'll be pretty from up there. You like the Ferris wheel."

"I'll stay down here with Katie. She's too little," Abby protested, the long evening finally getting to her.

"Katie is going with me," Jack piped up. "She doesn't want to miss anything, do you, Katie-girl?" He tossed her over his head, and she let out a squeal.

Abby forced both men and boys to swear. "Repeat after me. I will not rock the seat when it's stopped on or near the top. The way my stomach is feeling, someone on the bottom will be very sorry."

Nick and Jack exchanged pretend-thoughtful glares.

Jack teased. "I don't know. Katie likes to rock."

"Jack," Abby warned.

The bar was bolted in place, and their car rose a little and then stopped. For the next few minutes, the car would rise and stop while others were being loaded. Katie babbled and pointed, jabbered and rested back against her daddy's chest. Nick stretched to see more of everything, leaning forward occasionally to wave at people below. At every sway of the car, Abby grabbed Nick and made him sit back.

The night air was sharp and clear. As they neared the top, Abby was filled with that near-terror everyone feels when hanging on the edge of nowhere with nothing below you but luck. And at the same time, she was glad that she had climbed on. The sights and sounds were well worth the worry.

The lights beyond them were laid out in a crazy pattern. The sounds from below were amplified. The movements of people like ants, scurrying here and there. They rose, leaving the ground far below. Retreating from the world itself and capturing a piece of air all their own. Even if only temporarily.

The Ferris wheel, full with passengers now, began to rotate. Slowly at first and then faster. The lights became a smear, the music a wash of sound. Faster. The repetitive lift and fall of the stomach caused Abby to put a hand there.

Jack covered her hand with his. "Okay?" he yelled over the noise and whoosh of air.

"So far," she assured him, and reached over to kiss Katie's happy, shiny little face. Too young to know fear. How wonderful.

Nick and Ben sat on the other side of Jack and were too busy looking all around to see Jack plant a kiss on top of Abby's head as she leaned to kiss his daughter.

"Here—" he offered her a peppermint "—see if this will help your stomach."

It was too much. He couldn't help it. It was all too perfect. Like a real family on a real outing. Like husband and wife with brothers and sister sitting beside them. But it wasn't that way. It wasn't the truth. It was a lie. A play. A pretense. And right now he resented that it wasn't actuality. Other men were happily married. Some until they were ninety. What had he done to mess up his relationship? Where had he gone wrong?

He felt her relax for a moment and then jerk away

and sort of pivot a little to the other side. On the other ride a while ago, fires burned in him that he thought he'd banked for good. She called to him. All of him. And he wanted to answer. Would answer somehow.

It was a strong feeling. Almost savage. Here he was riding on a Ferris wheel, kids and other people all around, and all he could think of was taking her away to a dimly lit place...and making love with her all night long.

It's okay, Abby told herself. It was just a slipup. He had kissed the top of her head as he would Katie's. He probably hadn't even thought about it. It had just happened. She'd let it go. Better than bringing it up and then ending the conversation by asking him to move his mouth down a few inches.

Finally the ride slowed. The entire evening was coming to an end, and she didn't look forward to it. When they got home, she would make herself scarce and let Jack get the boys to bed. She needed some space and she needed it soon. If not, she might make a complete idiot of herself.

Their car stopped directly on top. It was beautiful. Serene. And scary.

Nick grinned and leaned forward slightly. "Look over there, Mom."

Abby grabbed the front of his shirt. "Be still. Sit back. Do not rock this car."

"Aw, Mom. Just a little."

"Let your mom enjoy the ride as much as you are, Nick. Boys are supposed to protect their moms, not tease them all the time."

"Aw, heck. Sure, Jack. I won't, Mom. But I want to."

"Well, I appreciate it, Nicky. It saves me from tying your legs in knots when we reach the ground."

Grinning devilishly, Jack began to move the car himself, just a little. Ben and Nick giggled as only little boys could.

She grabbed his shirtsleeve. "What are you doing?"

"I told Nick not to rock you. But I didn't promise not to."

Nick laughed outright as Jack continued to sway the car just the slightest bit. Ben hid his mirth behind his hand.

"You're at my mercy. What are you going to do? Get out?" He pretended a fiendish voice that had the kids laughing hysterically.

"I'll give you money," Abby said, playing along, adding the tone of a damsel in distress to her voice.

He rocked the car a little harder.

She put her hands over her heart and batted her eyelashes. "Oh, stop. Stop. I'll give you my house."

Jack twirled a pretend mustache. And rocked the car even more.

Abby grabbed the bar. "Okay. I'll give you the children."

Still using the voice of the villain, Jack chuckled. "Children, I have, I want you."

The words harpooned through her. Just the sound of them, even knowing it was all part of the game…it formed a picture, clear and bright, in her mind's eye. They were sitting close to each other. He raised his hands to cup her face and slowly lowered his face….

Just then, he swayed it too much, and she couldn't even pretend not to be scared out of her mind. She grabbed the front of Jack's shirt and held on, pressing her face to his shoulder.

"Game's over. Stop. Stop!"

Jack put his arm around her and laughed. "You're safe with me, lady. Look, even this baby girl isn't afraid when she's with me."

"That child doesn't know the meaning of fear. I do."

The Ferris wheel continued to move then stop, one car at a time, unloading passengers.

Jack was doing a good job with the boys. She had to respect that. She had to put a lid on the feelings she knew were developing for him. Like film in a darkroom, the picture was becoming all too clear.

All three of them laughed, and Katie reached her hands out toward the sky as if trying to catch a star.

Abby sighed. Content. Peaceful. And that was something she hadn't felt in a long, long time.

On the ground, they decided to go for one more ride and then home. The roller coaster. Abby adamantly and immediately declined and took Katie from Jack's arms. Jack, Ben and Nick ambled toward the curling, dipping, climbing, not-so-steady-looking conglomeration of painted-white two-by-fours. Abby headed for the drink stand and an ice-cold cup of cola.

Katie took a few sips and then instantly, like only a small child could, fell asleep in Abby's arms. She found an empty table and sat down.

It had been too long since she had held a sleeping babe in her arms. It felt good. Right. As if Katie belonged to her.

But she didn't. And this afternoon Jack had been on the phone with his workmen. He had slipped out to the building site while Katie napped and the boys were at a friend's house. His business would be financially square by the end of the summer. He may be ready to leave.

Abby waved to the men as the little train snaked its way up the first steep incline. Of course, all of them had their arms raised in the air as if the first swift, straight-down drop would do nothing to their fear glands. Abby crunched on the ice in her cola.

A short while later, the three of them came jogging from the ride, roughhousing and exchanging high fives. At that very moment, for a flash fire of a twinkling, Abby could have sworn she and Jack and the kids were really and truly one big, happy family.

It was the sorcery of the night, for the image disappeared as quickly as it had appeared. Abra. Cadabra. Poof!

The jabbering males purchased colas and paper cones filled to overflowing with boardwalk fries and returned to the picnic table.

The boys were retelling every dip and climb, every curve and roll upside down to their mother. Both boys' mouths were going at one time.

Jack sat across from Abby. The bright, many-colored lights shone behind her, lighting her hair to flame. She listened intently to each kid, even though exhaustion was evident on her face, smiling in disbelief and patting them on their backs for their bravado.

He wanted that perfect, busy hand on his back. He wanted to pull that hand to his lips. Turn the palm out and lay his mouth there. He wanted to watch realization dawn in her eyes. As the music from the carousel mixed with that of the calliope, he had the urge to go to her, pull her into his arms and dance her out into the circle of darkness surrounding the activity.

Just then, she glanced his way and smiled. He wanted to clear the picnic table with one swipe of his hand and take her, here and now.

If they were a family, that's probably exactly what would happen when they got home.

They would all wearily but happily climb the stairs and put the kids to bed. No baths, just one of those nights when you're drop-dead tired and cleanliness doesn't come into the picture. The kids would fall asleep fast. The house would go from complete turmoil and noise to peace and quiet in seconds. He would hear the sound of water running in the bathroom. He would drop his clothes outside the door and then quietly walk in.

Pushing aside the shower curtain, he would see her there, head back beneath the fall of steaming water. She would sense he was there and merely hold out her hands for him to join her. She would welcome him.

They would come together, hot water cascading, like standing under a waterfall. He would slick her body with soap, and she would curl into his hands.

Her milky white shoulders, the long column of her throat. The soap bubbles would slide across her breasts, down her rib cage and lower. He would follow them with his tongue.

She would murmur his name as she traced her hands along his body, leaving scalding trails behind. She would wind her arms around his neck, and her legs around his waist. He would lean forward and...

"Come on, Jack, we're leaving." Abby burst through his fantasy. "Where were you?"

Jack shook his head, saying nothing, and led the way to the parking lot. Katie didn't stir as he lifted her from Abby's arms and shifted her to his shoulder. She wouldn't even wake up when he dumped her into bed and slipped her shoes off.

Everyone was beat. A good kind of tired. The crowd was thinning out now, and the parking lot was emptying as cars and trucks pulled out in a long line toward the road. They joined the weary exodus of people from the lot.

His arm slipped over Abby's shoulder, and he slowed his pace to match hers. She turned her face up to thank him for a great evening and never even thought to stop him as she saw his mouth coming closer. She never knew where her next footstep would take her. She didn't even give it a thought as his lips sealed over hers in a short, sweet, mind-bending kiss.

For a moment, her mind went blank. The night was dark. There seemed to be no one else around, and there was complete silence. Only the sound of her own blood rushing through her veins filled her ears. And then reality slipped back in.

"First one to spot the van can be the last one to bed when we get home." It was an old joke, since they had forgotten the location of their own van several times in simple places like grocery-store parking lots and theater lots. And before the sentence was completely out of her mouth, she realized it was a line used by Jim to the boys. She could have bitten her tongue off.

Turning to try to joke that line away, she ruffled Nick's hair and then reached for Ben. She groped nothing but air.

He wasn't there.

She came to an abrupt halt, nearly causing Jack to fall over her. Walking a circle around all of them, she grabbed hold of Nick. There was no other little boy close by.

"Where's Ben? Ben!" she shouted, the instant panic evident in her voice.

Everyone stopped.

Terror squeezed her heart.

"Did you see Ben walk off?" She had a death grip on Nick.

"No, Mom, he was right beside me."

Abby whirled and took off running back toward the lights. "Ben! Ben!" She shouted at the top of her lungs as she ran between parked cars and toward the fairway.

Her little baby! Oh, God, she had let him down again. It was her job to protect him. To see all. To be all. Instead, she was leaning against Jack and pleasing herself.

She had failed again. Miserably.

Chapter Eight

Her baby! How could this happen? He'd been right there. They were all watching him.

"Ben! Ben!"

Jack grabbed her by the arm and swung her around. "It's not going to do any good to go running helter-skelter. You'll end up lost, too. I'll find him."

She pulled away and made it a few more steps before he stopped her again. "You're in a panic. I'm not going to have you running in front of a moving car or passing out on us. Stay here."

"Like hell." There was fire in her eyes and anger at herself in her heart. "He's my kid, not yours. And you lost him!"

Her words cut through him sharp as a rapier. He hadn't expected that. Her look of panic and terror sliced his heart. But it was her words, her accusation, that had him bleeding.

Boys were boys. They'd find him. That's what he told himself as he sprinted forward, moving to circle the perimeter of the fairground, Nick at his side, Katie in his arms. He'd be fine. He would. He had to be.

She powered past them and into the leaving crowd. She ignored the startled stares and the over-the-shoulder looks cast her way. She searched every young face, looking for her child.

She was a bad mother. The words rolled over and over in her head. She should have had his hand. She shouldn't have taken her eyes off of him. Not in this crowd. She should have made them both march along in front of her.

She was losing her mind with every second that passed and she couldn't spot him. Perspiration rolled down her forehead and into her eyes. Her muscles cramped, and a stitch in her side threatened to slow her down. She felt light-headed and fought the urge to pass out. Tears now joined the sweat that streaked her face. People moved to her, asked questions, but she couldn't say anything but her son's name. Others joined the search now, stopped in their trek to their cars by the plight of this hysterical, crying woman.

She tripped and went down on her knees. Someone helped her up, and she was running again. The lights were no longer awesome but threatening. The music was no longer wonderful but mocking. The cool night air was no longer bracing but freezing. The rides were no longer the promise of a thrill but huge monsters aggressive enough to strike down her little boy.

Even hiring Jack hadn't guaranteed safety. What would? How could she lose her own child? Her brain stripped of all reasoning, her heart breaking, Abby darted here and there looking at every child, diving into every dark corner calling Ben's name.

She couldn't breathe. The night sky began to whirl,

and she felt as if she were being sucked into a vortex, her arms pinned to her sides no matter how hard she tried to reach out. She heard Ben's voice calling to her. She prayed this was a nightmare and she would wake up. Any minute now, she would sit straight up in bed and wake up. Ben and Nick would be safe and sound in their own beds.

Where else to look? Behind the tent. Under the hay wagon. Oh, God, had he gone back to see the elephants one more time? She headed for the outskirts of the lot, tripped over a guide wire and fell. Getting up, the pain in her knee sharp and distinct, she turned.

And then she saw them. Striding through the thinning crowd. Jack wore a huge grin on his face; Katie having grown sleepy, rested her head on his shoulder. Nick was on one side, and little Ben walked at his other side. And that damn puppy was in Ben's hands and tucked under his chin.

Jack Murdock had found her child. Jack Murdock was bringing him safely back to her. In that split second, she saw him in a light she'd never been exposed to before, and she felt such a strong emotion rip through her chest for the man. Gratitude. That's all it could be. He was her knight in shining armor. Her son was safe! The anger, the resentment, she felt for him in a moment of panic vanished.

The world spun. Her vision blurred. Abby fainted, her legs unable to hold her any longer.

When she came to, she was in Jack's arms and Ben was at their side. Nick was holding Katie's hand, and they were walking through the parking lot, the Kid Kab in sight.

She reached down and squeezed one of Ben's

hands. Then wiggled in Jack's arms. "I'm all right now. Let me down."

"You are not. Keep still, damn it."

He tightened his grip on her and forced her to stay where she was. Weakened, she let it be. Her head rolled against his arm, and her cheek rested on his chest. She could hear the steady thump of his heart, air move in and out of his lungs. She liked the feel of his arms under her legs, of her hip resting against his belt buckle.

Oh, God, Ben was safe. She was safe. She closed her eyes and went out again.

He watched her.

She hadn't stirred as the Kid Kab arrived home with everyone inside safe and sleepy. She hadn't budged when he carried her upstairs to her room and laid her across her bed. He'd never seen anyone in such a state before, but he knew how he would have felt had it been Katie. Abby had completely worn herself out. She'd called down many more horrors into her imagination than she needed to, he knew. He left her then, to put the kids to bed.

No baths tonight. Just a little of the pink liquid for Nick's stomach, a warm washcloth got rid of most of the candy remains from Katie's mouth and hands and Ben managed to get his shoes off before dropping into deep sleep over his bedspread.

And the puppy. The little innocent ball of fur that caused this entire mess was curled up against Ben's leg, fast asleep and, like Ben, totally unaware of the trouble he'd caused that night.

Now, exhausted himself, Jack showered and pulled on clean jeans. Sitting in the rocking chair beside her bed, his bare feet propped on her mattress, he watched over her.

His fingers itched to smooth down her hair that spread wildly across the pillow. His mouth wanted to wander across her tear-streaked cheeks and erase the traces of her distress. He wanted to know what it would feel like, having her curled up next to him. He wanted to spend his days seeing to it that she never felt alone and panicky again.

What was happening to him? After his divorce, he'd become hardened and bitter. He felt none of that now. Not in this house. Not with her around. His daughter loved her—of that he was certain. Even that didn't worry him. Katie would always have a relationship with Abby even when this arrangement came to an end. And it did have to come to an end. Someday.

She was dreaming. Fitful. Probably reliving the whole nightmare over in her exhaustion-induced sleep. Panic had shot adrenaline through her system. Relief had let her down too swiftly. Collapse was the best thing for her right now.

What was the best thing for him? She had screamed out that it was his fault. And it was. To a point. No one can see all, hear all and be all. Maybe higher beings should have given out that gift as they gave out the children, but they didn't.

And it had all worked out okay. He rubbed the bridge of his nose between his thumb and forefinger. He wouldn't let himself think about what would be happening right now if it hadn't. She was going to blame him no matter what. No matter that it was just a thing that happens. All parents do their best to avoid it, but things do happen. They were lucky it all turned out all right.

He'd take her anger and let her get over it. With everything else she had to deal with, there was no sense in making her share the guilt. It was best if the whole damn thing was just dropped and not spoken of again.

She thrashed about wildly and let out a cry. At first he let her be, wanting her to drive all the demons from her system. But when she didn't stop even after rapping her hand hard on the headboard, he dived for the bed and grabbed her wrists.

"It's okay, Abby," he soothed. "You're home. Ben's home. Wake up. You're just dreaming."

She continued to roll around for a few seconds until she began to come awake slowly. Her breathing was labored. Her eyes went wide. She sat straight up and moved to swing her legs over the edge of the bed to run.

Jack caught her, pushed her back against the mattress and flung a leg over hers. "Quit. Everything's okay. Ben's asleep in his bed. You're going to give me a black eye."

He felt every muscle in her body go lax. But not trusting her just yet, he kept a tight hold on her wrists and only moved his leg from over hers. That being a move to save himself more than her.

Sheer willpower kept him from climbing up in the bed beside her, gathering her in his arms, rocking her back and forth and kissing the fear away.

Blurry. The universe was soft and soaking her up. Foggy. The air was hard to breathe. Almost as if she were underwater. She couldn't see clearly. Unable to move her arms, she gave up the struggle. Warm, hard fingers curled around her wrists. Who?

She opened her eyes again. The events of the evening came crashing down on her.

"Ben!"

Jack caught her as she moved to slide from the bed. He knew she would have to see for herself. "Come on." He took her hand and put a supporting arm around her waist.

Shaky, Abby let Jack lead her down the hall, stood next to him as he quietly opened the child's door and led her to his bedside.

She knelt down and smoothed her hand over his hair and his cheek. He stirred and rolled over. Tears began to make their way down Abby's cheek when she saw the puppy against the foot of the bed.

Jack reached down and helped her up. She leaned against him. He picked her up as he would Katie and carried her back to her room, letting her get the crying part over with.

He set her on her feet near her bed. She steadied herself but she didn't back away from him. Jack needed her to.

"Thanks for finding Ben tonight."

"Let's not talk about it." Feeling guilty about his longing, he stepped back.

"I was mean to you."

"You were scared."

She looked up at him through tortured eyes. "I was to blame, too."

"For heaven's sake, Abby, no one is to blame. Take a shower. You'll feel better."

"Yes." Still in a bit of an exhaustion-influenced trance, she walked toward the shower.

Against his better judgment, he allowed his instincts to take over. "I'll wait here till you're safe in bed."

"No. I'm okay. I don't want you waiting here in my room."

That insulted him. After all they had been through tonight, she had to throw one more indignity his way.

"Damn it, as a friend. Okay, as your employee hired to see that all is well. That's my job. And that's it. I'm divorced, remember. I know I'm no catch. You surely don't think I have a sinister reason behind it. I certainly wouldn't set some lady up to feel something for me when I know I don't know how to maintain a good relationship. Damn it, woman."

She sobered with his outburst. She had obviously pushed one of his buttons. She stopped and walked back toward him. "Who told you that nonsense? I've seen you with the kids, with other people. There's no doubt in my mind that you'll make some woman a good husband. One who wants one."

"Oh, yeah, I must have been good at it. My wife left, didn't she? I'm here because my marriage dissolved into nothing. She walked out on me without even saying goodbye. I wasn't even worth that courtesy as a husband."

"You're too smart to say a stupid thing like that. Were you faithful to her?"

"Yes, I was that," he answered, wondering where that question came from.

"My husband was wonderful to me. Great with the boys. The model of what every husband and father should be." When he moved to say something, she held up a hand to stop him and went to sit on the edge of the bed.

"I told you Jim died in a car crash and that he was having an affair. A couple of weeks after the funeral, I went to Roberts International to get his personal belongings from the office. I shouldn't have done that. You know, now that I think back, if I hadn't done that maybe I would never have had to see proof of it. Never had to face it. I probably would have always wondered...but I would never have known the scope of it."

She shook her head. "Well, anyway I did. While I was gathering his things from his desk drawers, I started coming across pictures. Of Jim with a blonde at the beach. Of Jim with a brunette at a restaurant. Of Jim with a redhead at a dance club. Of Jim with his secretary on a hike in the mountains."

Old wounds that had begun to heal now ripped open and bled. He leaned forward in the rocking chair to touch her, and she stopped him. He sat back.

"Oh, there were pictures of me with Jim, too. The boys with their dad. And that made it all the worse. I was just one more in a long line." She let her head fall into her hands.

"Stop. It's over. Don't do this to yourself."

She laughed a little. "We're a pair, aren't we? You'll never trust another woman, and I'll never trust another man. Yet here we are asking each other for help nearly every day."

"We have every reason to feel that way."

"Reason doesn't come into it. Sometimes when I think back on all that, I hate him so much. Because I loved him and he had me convinced that he loved me. We were a happy family. The boys worshiped him and he them. He fooled me. He used me. How could I have been so wrong?"

"I'm sure he did love you and the boys. The other stuff, well, it was only other stuff. How can a man be around you and not love you?"

The open-ended question hung in the air between them. It warmed her heart, his sideways compliment. She wanted to thank him for it but couldn't. "What caused your divorce? Do you even know?"

"No. She just lost interest. I guess I didn't do some things I should have done."

"You'll never know for sure, maybe, but I'd bet you aren't as much at fault as you think you are. You're a great guy, Jack. If you're the same man today you were when you were with her, she was the fool. There's no reason for a woman to leave you."

She scrubbed at her face with both hands. "I'm so tired. I'm going to take that shower now. Thanks for talking awhile. And thanks again for finding my son."

He nodded as she moved toward the bathroom again.

She closed the door.

He waited.

The light from the bathroom behind her, Abby padded toward her bed with a huge, snowy white towel wrapped around her. It was then she saw him there. Asleep in the rocker. Waiting.

Toweling her long, curly hair dry, she sat on the bed in front of Jack and took this unnoticed moment in the half-light to really look at him.

He was definitely a gentleman. Most definitely a protector. He was sweet and sharp, funny and giving. If she let herself, she could fall so madly in love with this guy...but she wouldn't. By God, she wouldn't. They had a good friendship, and she felt the need to protect it. Jim's infidelities had left her with a very strong distrust of men. Of everyone, actually. She didn't think she would ever allow herself to become vulnerable to another person. And being in love left you exactly that.

For a while she had blamed herself for Jim's infidelity. She'd thought she'd been lacking somewhere. But she knew she'd been a good wife. Jim must have had his own reasons for cheating—reasons that had nothing to do with her. Still, the pain of betrayal cut deep.

Jack stirred and opened his eyes. She was beautiful. Rosy and damp, her long hair curling in tendrils over her shoulders as she worked at it with a towel. Her shoulders were bare. The rise of her breasts, lovely above the towel. He wanted to run his fingers there.

Abby opened her mouth to say good-night and order him from her room. Instead, she became speechless as he simply reached forth and lifted her to his lap. Taking the towel from her, he took over drying her hair.

It was a dream. That's why she didn't stop him. It wasn't real. That's why when she moved her lips, no words came out. It was one of those patches in time that belonged nowhere and to no one.

Floating, yet anchored to the solid hardness of his torso, she waited in a mist as he ran the towel over her hair. This is wrong, a small voice echoed in the hollows of her mind. It's right, a loud voice answered from the core of her heart.

She curled there in his lap, like his Katie would. He rocked back and forth, back and forth. The act was to comfort, nothing else. And she needed solace right now. Tomorrow she would probably be sorry she had let them get this close. Tomorrow she would worry about it.

He dropped the towel to the floor in a white pool. Her heart thudded hard against her rib cage. Time stood still.

His fingers rubbed her scalp. Slow, lazy circles that caused her head to drop back in his hands. Down her neck, the massage continued, slow, languorous, seductive. Across her shoulders, down her arms and up again.

He caught her chin and turned her face toward his. In the shadowy light, from beneath closing lids, she could see his face. So close. So very close. She could feel the heat from his skin. The light brush of his breath.

Intoxicating. Hypnotizing. His lips were below her ear. Soft. Tantalizing. Across her cheek. Smooth. Warm.

He waited. Invited. Promised. Gave them both a chance to turn back. She twisted into the kiss.

Mouth crushed mouth. No gentleness here. Only heat and haste and hunger.

Electricity that tingled in her stomach now bolted across her body like lightning. She couldn't get enough, fast enough.

His tongue dived in to taste, and she answered with her own. He changed the angle of the kiss, lips sliding across lips, teeth nipping.

The drugging effect of need slowed her down and then drove her faster. Her mind was stripped of all reason. Her body was consumed with desire and asking no permission.

There was so much to feel, so much to experience. Where had all these emotions been hiding? How had she lived all her life without feeling the mix of them? Not even with Jim...

He had been sure it would be like this. The silkiness, the smoothness, the roughness, the heat. She consumed him; she took him over. Filled his brain. Shoved all thought and reason from him. There was no room for anything or anyone but her. Only her.

She pulled him even closer, her arms tightening around his neck. Soon, soon there would be no turning back. No stopping. He picked her up, their mouths still locked in a kiss, and laid her on the bed. He waited for her to resist. To tell him to stop. She didn't.

As his lips explored the skin at her shoulder, her neck, her arms and the curves above the towel, his hands discovered the satiny softness of her thigh, behind her knee, her ankle.

A soft moan escaped her lips, only to be captured by his. He raised his hand to the knot that held the towel securely around her and pulled it loose.

He rolled, pulling her on top of him, the towel left behind. The burn of flesh upon flesh and flesh upon denim soared up through her and threatened to consume her. Absolutely nothing had ever felt this good in her entire life. She wanted him. And wanted him now.

He reached for the snap on his jeans.

"Oh, Abby."

The sound of her name groaned from his lips brought reality crashing down around her. She wanted him. Oh yes, she did. But it would change things. Complicate them. Endanger them. And she needed him, needed things to stay the same for the sake of the kids. And for herself, she realized almost too late. If she gave her body to him tonight, her heart followed. And she had sworn never to give it again. She pulled away.

He pulled her back.

"Don't, Jack. Stop. I'm sorry. Please."

"I want you," he breathed heavily. "You want me."

"Yes. Yes, I do. But I'm not going to."

He held her tightly for a few heated moments and then let go of her, his arms flopping out to his sides.

It took all of her willpower, but she rolled off of him and pulled the towel around her. Sitting on the edge of the bed, she regained her composure, a little sliver at a time.

She heard his heavy breathing, turned to look at him. He was beautiful stretched out on the bed. She wanted absolutely nothing more than to lie back down with him.

"I'm sorry," she whispered.

He moved to the other side of the bed, dropped his feet to the floor and stood up.

He stood there for a few seconds, quietly and a bit unsteadily. Then, without a word, he strode from the room.

Abby let the towel fall away as she pushed the spread back and climbed into bed. It was still warm where their bodies had entwined. All this had happened because of the events of the evening. She had needed comforting; he had needed assurance that she wasn't blaming him. That made sense, didn't it?

More sense than the feeling that they were both falling in love. The two of them. Both sworn off the opposite sex. Things always seemed different at night. In the light of day, they would both forget tonight and be glad it hadn't followed through to the end. She might be falling in love, but how would she ever know, really know if he was feeling the same thing? If he was even capable of it?

That thought was no comfort as she slipped into a deep, dissipated sleep.

Something woke her. It was still dark, but there was noise in the hallway. Groggy from exhaustion, mental and physical, she slipped into a robe and moved quietly to open the door.

Jack was in the hall, a hand on Ben's little shoulder as they walked toward the stairs that led down to the kitchen. Ben was sniffing. Was he crying? She started to bolt out into the hall to find out, but something stopped her. As soon as the two males disappeared down the stairway, she gave them a few minutes and then followed.

A soft light lit the stairwell from the kitchen. She heard the sounds of the refrigerator being opened up and...what was that? Oh, yes, the lid from the peanut-butter jar spinning. They were eating again? Her stomach lurched.

She could hear their voices but not make out what they were saying. She moved forward a little just to be sure nothing was wrong, and the voices became clearer as Abby heard Ben speak.

"You really think it was Dad that let you find me? I didn't see him. And I was awful lost."

Abby sat heavily on the stairs, her head leaning against the wall. She pulled her knees up and hugged her arms around them. A tear rolled down her cheek.

"Remember when we were talking about angels? Guardian angels. I think your dad is yours. The way I got it figured, he sort of pushed me and tugged me in the right direction so I'd see you behind that generator.''

"Really?" Ben's little voice was full of hope.

"Sure. You want some jelly on this sandwich?"

"Yeah. I didn't see him anywhere."

"You can't see them, but you can feel them in here. In your heart. No one wants to die, Benny. No one. And your dad didn't even have time to come back and say goodbye. Accidents happen quick. I know it's hard for you to understand."

"I watch 'Rescue 911.'"

"So then you do know how bad things happen even when people try not to let it. But I know your dad still loves you. Wherever he is. And hey, you'll see him again someday when you're an angel."

"Me. Hey, yeah. I don't know. I don't want to wear a dress or nothing. And carrying that harp around ain't much fun."

Jack's laugh was full and hearty. "Come here and give me a hug, Ben. I'll put in a word about changing the angel dresses to jeans."

Abby had to put a hand over her mouth to keep to herself the sob that tore through her throat.

"I love you, Ben." Jack ventured the words slowly.

After a second, Ben sighed. "Me, too," he admitted quietly.

"Anytime you want to talk, man-to-man, you just let me know."

"Well, Mom keeps saying that we have to remember that you and Katie might be leaving one day."

"That's true. Right now we all need each other to make life easier and happier. Someday we may not. But that doesn't mean that we don't love each other just because we don't live together. We can still do things. Go places. Pitch ball. Sit down and watch a movie. We'll always be friends and love each other."

"Promise?"

"Yes. That promise I can make if you can remember that to love somebody you don't have to be with them every day. Do you understand that?"

"Like loving Grandma and Grandpa even though they live in Florida?"

"That's it."

"It still would be much better if they were here all the time."

"I know."

Ben was silent a minute and then he asked Jack, "After you put in a word about the angel pants, could you ask Mom to let me keep Nemo?"

"Nemo?"

"The dog."

"I like that name. I'll talk to Mom. Now, eat your sandwich so we can both go back to bed. It's still nighttime."

Abby gathered her gown and crept silently back up the stairs. This was time for the two of them to share alone. Sunshine had broken through Ben's cloudy days, and Jack had done it. He was solely responsible for getting to the core of the little boy. For reaching in and touching him. Saving him.

Sunday morning dawned dreary. Everyone had slept late. Abby awoke to the smell of coffee. As she approached the kitchen, she heard the sound of bacon frying in the pan. She felt as if she'd fallen under a semi and been dragged forty miles.

Laughter reached her ears. The happy yelping of a canine did, too.

She was embarrassed to face Jack, but the sooner done, the sooner over with. And how would she be able to keep from smiling when she saw Ben and Jack together and remembered all their words to each other? She could never give away that she knew.

She pasted a smile on her face and entered the kitchen. "Morning, everybody. We all slept late. It's nearly eleven."

Jack looked up from the morning paper, put it down and got up to fix her a cup of coffee. He looked like hell. She guessed he hadn't slept at all last night. She couldn't remember a time in her life when a man had lost sleep over her. She had this weird urge to walk to him and lay a kiss on his stubbled cheek. Smooth his uncombed hair. Run her fingers across his wide, hard shoulders.

"Sit. I'll fix it, thanks," she answered lightly even though she felt anything but carefree.

"It's my job," he said thunderously, and went on to prepare it for her.

"Your job is to care for the boys. I can do for myself."

"You and Jack fighting, Mom?" Nick asked between mouthfuls of toast, grinning.

"Not yet," Abby answered good-naturedly, and smiled at Jack. It was painful. The entire episode, but they had to get through the first awkward moments.

She baited them. "What's to be done with the dog?"

Ben looked up at her, his eyes wide with innocence. "Why, Mom, we're going to keep him, aren't we, Nick? Nick said he'll help me take care of him. You don't have to do nothing."

"Very thoughtful of you both, but I don't know about this. Someone may be looking for their little lost puppy right this minute."

Jack grumbled from behind the paper. "Carnival's a good place to dump a puppy and be sure he finds a good home."

"I'd say somebody needs a nap already."

The boys roared with laughter as Jack looked over the newspaper one more time.

Abby was ravenous. She felt all woman and ready to conquer the world this morning. Was all this a result of the depth of Jack's wanting her last night?

Jack got up, turned the bacon and sat back down, feigning interest in the paper once more. He'd be damned if he'd let her know he had rolled and turned all night. That the remembrance of her at his fingertips tingled through him even now. That the strong urge to throw her to the floor was strangling him.

The bacon popped. He got up and forked it over to paper towels and began breaking eggs into the grease.

"Good grief, Jack. Drain some of the grease before you cook these things."

"They'll be fine. Taste better this way."

The children, finished with their cereal and toast, took the dog outside and raced around the backyard.

Abby was being overly cheerful, and Jack was being overly grumpy. Where would all this get them?

"Come on, Jack. Let's start over."

Jack studiously folded the paper and then drained the last of his coffee without looking at her.

He sighed. Resigned to working things out even though at times it didn't seem beneficial, he nodded.

He reminded himself that it was helping the kids that he had to keep in mind. The fact that his ego had been smashed to the floor last night shouldn't bother him in the least.

"Dallas called early this morning. Vandals tore down most of the second floor of a house they're working on in Shepherdstown."

"That's too bad."

"Not to mention costly. If you're going to be here all day, I'll take a ride over there and inspect that entire project. See if I can pick up on any reason for sabotage."

"Sabotage? Oh, a mystery. Can't we all come along?"

He hadn't even thought of taking them all over there and exposing them to any danger that might be lurking.

"I don't think so. This isn't some Sunday-afternoon outing."

"Okay. No big deal. And Jack—" she couldn't help poking fun at him "—there's no reason to keep that darn puppy."

He glanced at her before he stood up to go outside. "There's no reason not to. But you can tell Ben he has to take the dog back. To where? The carnival? The dog pound?"

"That's not fair, Jack."

"All kids want a dog. I had one. A mixed breed, a mongrel, but he was always there with me."

Can't get off the hook that easily, she thought and said, "He'll die someday."

He laughed and shook his head. "Let's just hope Ben has grown up enough by then to accept it. Are you going to put him in a plastic bubble all his life and protect him from everything that might hurt him?''

"Would if I could," she answered, her chin jutting upward.

"Think about it. You wouldn't. Think of all he'd miss. You can't tell the bad times from the good if you never have the bad."

He walked to the screen and watched the children playing in the yard. They were trying to teach the puppy to fetch, but instead, Katie would burst forth and try to catch the ball.

"Look here." He motioned for Abby to join him at the doorway.

Absently he dropped an arm around her shoulder. "No one could ask for more than this."

"Thank you, Jack."

"For what?"

"Everything. Nothing." She wanted to tell him about overhearing their conversation last night. She wanted to thank him for pulling Ben the rest of the way into the future and out of the past. But she knew that his and Ben's conversation had to remain between her two men. Slip of the tongue...the mental tongue. Her one little man and...

They stood there, the two of them, just like any old married couple on a Sunday morning, watching their kids laugh and play in the backyard. Abby leaned over and kissed Jack on the cheek.

Except that they weren't, Abby thought, and that was a shame.

Jack pulled the truck out of the driveway a little while later. For the first time in weeks, Abby was going to have the house and the kids all to herself.

She had lots of ideas rolling around in her head. Laundry was in the washing machine, beds made, dinner was simmering in the Crock-Pot and…she was lonely.

The realization came to her as she sat on the lounge in the backyard watching the kids run that poor puppy to death. She didn't like being alone. She had grown so used to having Jack around that she hadn't even noticed it. Was she beginning to have faith again, to depend on someone else after all?

She went back to her notes. Life was going to be easy at Ye Olde Flower Shoppe. Part of it was due to the humor Jack seemed to bring to every problem that faced him. She vowed to follow his advice on how to handle some situations, finding that the man had a talent for problem solving.

But missing Jack? She sat back in her chair and chewed on the end of her pen. Somehow her concentration had been interrupted and had changed course. Along with seeing to the boys' needs, she had begun to indulge in a little fantasy with Jack. This had to stop. It could certainly go nowhere. Jack didn't want to marry and settle down again. She sure as heck didn't.

She'd throw herself into her work and into her boys' lives and try to get some distance between herself and Jack again. She didn't like this feeling of missing him, of needing him. And she was determined to get it under control while she still could.

Katie fell and the puppy jumped all over her, slathering her with his wet tongue. Katie laughed at first, and then when Ben and Nick didn't get him off of her fast enough, she began to cry.

Nap time. Abby went into the house and ran water

on a washcloth and took it back outside. Gathering Katie up, she washed away any doggy germs and headed back for the house.

"Hey, you guys, toss me that ball as soon as I come back from putting missy here to bed. We'll play some dodgeball."

She laughed as the screen door bounced shut behind her. It struck her as funny. Dodgeball. It seemed that was just another term for life.

Chapter Nine

Jack flipped through the pages of the gardening book he'd just smuggled home from the library. Between the fertilizer section and the hints on how to plant tree seedlings, he found himself thinking about his new family unit. They were just the answer, especially after his failed marriage and his determination not to lose himself to another doomed relationship again. He had it all. A pseudo-wife, a woman who definitely loved his little girl, a beautiful house to live in, a paycheck, time to get his business together. The rest...what simmered between them was purely physical. Wasn't it? And hadn't they been dealing with it every day?

Potting soil. Chapter nine.

Pulling into the driveway, Abby turned the wheel tightly to avoid smashing a red toy dump truck. She sighed and sat back in the seat. Home. Adjustments. She made them. He made them. The kids made them.

She had fallen so close to proclaiming her feelings for Jack after the night he and Ben talked, that she had now gone almost completely the other way.

Ever since that night at the carnival, over a month ago, when Ben had gotten lost chasing that mongrel puppy, the newest addition to the household, he had moved a lot closer to living in the here and now. Abby could tell Ben still held on to thoughts of his dad, but he was accepting. A little at a time.

He still held back some but he did include Jack in his day-to-day activities. He didn't pout nearly as much. He was beginning to look forward to every day and small events. And Abby was grateful to Jack. The flower shop had its place in healing Ben. He was becoming more and more outgoing talking with the customers. Abby even found him offering his six-year-old advice to an elderly man shopping for a gift for his wife yesterday.

Even though she made sure that everyone involved remembered that this living arrangement might just be a temporary situation, she began to feel unsure that she herself could handle it if it turned out that way. Had she already begun to consider this to be her world? They had fallen into a routine, and even though it smacked very much of a happily married couple and their kids, the other part, the intimate part, was kept at arm's length where it was safer.

Abby retrieved the two bags of groceries from the trunk and headed for the back door. She pushed it open with her elbow and kicked it shut with one foot. No one had heard her drive up and come out to help. Plus, she was a little perturbed that her mind had been on Jack all day. Okay, so she didn't trust herself either. She was lonely and he was such a big help. A bright spot in everyone's life. He was always happy and never tiring. The boys were blossoming like hothouse flowers, she chuckled to herself, under his love and guidance. If she found herself yearning for a little tender loving care herself...well, wasn't that just natural? It didn't mean anything. It surely didn't mean that she and Jack were beginning to have any real, any lifetime-dependable feelings for each other. He was too perfect, and she was sick of thinking of it at all!

He was a beautiful sight standing here in her kitchen, his hair uncombed. The dark T-shirt was slit under his arms to his waist. She'd bet his skin was warm. She realized she had a strong urge to walk over to him, slide her hands through the openings in his shirt and feel every inch of him.

She shuffled toward the counter and shoved the bags on top just in time to keep from dropping them all over the floor. The decided clunk got his attention.

He slapped the book closed and slid it behind him. "I'll put that stuff away in a minute."

One hand on the counter and one at her hip, she smiled smugly. "What do you have behind you?"

He feigned innocence. "Nothing."

"Jack."

He backed away from her toward the stairs. "One of the kids' books. They left it on the porch. I was taking it back to their room."

She held out her hand as she would to one of her boys when he was being uncooperative. "Let me see it."

He cocked his head. "No." Swinging the book in front of him, he turned and jogged toward the steps.

She ran after him and dodged in front. Jumping for

the book with both hands, she wrenched it free and held it out in front of her.

"One Hundred and One Easy-to-Grow Species of Flowers and Plants?" It melted her to butter. A large, bright pool at his feet. It touched her heart where it had never ever been touched before. Right at the very core.

"That is so sweet. I don't believe you took the time to check out a book to learn about the business. You said you didn't like puttering around with green things."

"I've got to put the cold stuff away." He turned on his heel and swaggered back to the kitchen.

"You said the only thing dirt was good for was walking on." She put the book down on the kitchen table and followed him. She came around the counter and took his hand, the one hoisting the peanut butter to the top shelf. She took the jar from him and set it down.

"You said that your hands were too big to handle tiny flowers." Holding his wrist, she turned his hand, palm up. She had the wildest urge to bring it to her lips.

Something inside of her told her not to make this kind of contact with him again. But something in the way he looked down at her, challenged her, made her walk into his arms.

As soon as she was within an inch of him, her dark, warm scent, the feel of her soft yet firm body beneath his hands, had him realizing he was making a mistake. A big one. One he wouldn't correct if his life depended on it.

She had a nearly undeniable urge to simply step forward and lean against him. She wanted, needed, to feel all of him against all of her. It was going to happen, one way or the other. She couldn't have prevented it. She slipped her arm up to his shoulder. "Can I have this dance?"

"Dance?" he questioned, completely caught off guard.

"You make me feel so special. You are such a different man. Dance with me right now, right here, or I'll do something really silly that we'll probably regret."

"I have absolutely no idea what you're talking about, but you got it, lady."

Foolishness, she told herself, and kept her distance as he smoothly and elegantly led her to the center of the kitchen to glide to the slow ballad that smoked across the airwaves of the radio sitting on top of the refrigerator.

Abby steeled herself against her feelings. This was just exactly what she had set out to avoid more than a year ago. And here she was. Wanting. Needing. Her brain trying to figure out how to handle this when her body seemed to be in control. Rational thoughts drifted away.

Jack wasn't a man inclined to regrets and he wouldn't start now. She was flame in his hands. She worked her way into his bloodstream effortlessly. He held her inches away from him so he could search her eyes as they smiled up at him.

Neither of them wanted a relationship with the other. Hadn't they been there before? Hadn't they discussed all this time and again? Yet here they were. Touching. Reaching out. Answering.

He laid his forehead against hers. "I can't resist you."

Abby didn't want it to end. "Right now, this moment, I don't want you to. This will be all, and then we'll simply go our separate ways."

He groaned, low in his throat. "It's not that simple."

"It has to be."

She couldn't have prevented it if she had been a magician. And that she certainly wasn't. He seemed so vulnerable. So in need of assurance. It was the gentle way he held her, the respectful way he kept the distance between them even though his body throbbed with need for her. The air all around them was voltaic, purely jumping with electricity. Her mind clouded, and her senses floated away. She took a step forward and brought their bodies to within a half inch of each other. And then she slowly looked up at him again.

He couldn't have stopped it if he wanted to. And he didn't. He brought her hard against him, forcing all the air from her lungs. Reaching up, he clasped the jeweled clip that held her hair in place on top of her head and released it, dropping it to the floor. Neither one heard the clatter. Her hair cascaded down around her shoulders and across his hands. He curled his fingers into it.

Dark. Heady. Sultry. In the silhouette of lovers, enhanced by time and history, he bent down and caught her mouth with his. His mouth was hot and hard. Demanding. Taking.

Surrendering. Conquering. Her mouth opened in accommodation, giving his tongue access to the hidden taste of her.

Fire spread through her limbs, heating the center of her. Her response to him was immediate...and primal.

Her arms wound around his neck. She went quickly beyond questioning to nothing. Only drifting. Feeling. Sinking. Good. So good.

He was solid and hot and yielding beneath her hands. He was a life preserver and she was drowning. She held on with both hands to keep from falling under the waves of passion as they swirled around her, increasingly insistent.

He straightened, lifting her off the floor. She was weightless, yet she filled him from head to foot. The taste of her, the smell of her, the feel of her. All encompassing. Like a hand inside a glove, she slipped inside his system.

He drew back, only an inch or so, and looked into her eyes. They were half-closed. Her mouth was swollen from his onslaught. He leaned forward and rubbed his lips across hers and heard her moan. A man could get lost in a woman like this. He could take days discovering his way and losing it again.

She could feel his heart thunder against her breasts. Her blood twirled and whirled through her veins at breakneck speed, dizzying her. She closed the small remaining space between them, the whisper's breadth, and heard the groan in his throat as she scraped her teeth across his bottom lip. Or was it her own growling that she heard, distant in her ears?

Her hands cruised his back and his shoulders; her fingers dived into his hair. So thick, so soft, so rough. She changed the angle of the kiss and met his tongue with her own.

Inferno. Willingly trapped inside the red-hot steel walls of passion.

He allowed her to slide back down his body, ever so slowly, inch by inch, reveling in each ridge and peak until her feet were beside his. His hands streaked up her sides, across her back and up to cup her face, increasing the pressure of mouth to mouth.

If this was madness, then let her be insane. If this was wrong, then lock her up and throw away the key. Imprison her. Banish her, as long as it was with him. She wanted to fall to the floor with him. She craved. She coveted. She thirsted.

Never had a woman streamed into his entire being before, like helium into a balloon. Never had a woman flowed through his system, hot and heady, lethal as poison. It tore away restraints. Bashed down barriers. He had sworn off all women. And he would keep that sacred oath, except for Abby. His Abby. The words burned through him like a blaze of flaming arrows.

Oh, God, he wouldn't stay here, not when it could go no farther. Couldn't. They could have handled anything. Anything but this…raw hunger…this over-whelming need…this insatiable want. Now he had to have her, and there was no turning back.

She felt the difference in him. He was backing off. Pushing her away. Slowly she became aware of her surroundings. The room was bright from the after-noon sun. The children were playing right outside the window. He held her tightly against him, while his breathing slowed and he forced himself under control. She clung to him, lost as to what had changed.

He left her there and went back to filling the shelves.

She waited a good long while until the trembling stopped. "What's happening to us?"

"Nothing. It's just proximity. And loneliness. We're man and woman in a strange situation. I'm sorry. I know you don't want a relationship with a man again. Although that's not what you were saying a second ago in my arms.''

Hurt. Indignant, she slammed a cupboard door and headed for the stairs. "Men don't usually say they're sorry after they kiss me." Men don't usually kiss me, she thought foolishly as she made her way up the steps.

He had to leave, Jack told himself. How could he continue under the same roof with her, knowing that she was only a few doors down the hall, sleeping? The thought of stalking down the dimly lit passageway and opening the door to her room… He scrubbed at his face with his hands as he made his way to the liquor cabinet. Pouring two fingers of whiskey, he downed it in one gulp.

He would hate putting Katie in day care. Maybe he should move out West so his mom could care for her. No, he knew his mother would if she could, but she was older now and not able to keep up with a toddler. Katie was his to raise.

Nick and Ben would be mad at him for a while, disappointed, but he would make it a point to come over and do things with them on weekends and maybe even once during the week. Little Benny. He'd finally just come around that corner and was able to show his affection openly for Jack. They'd talked just the other day, sort of man-to-man, about stuff. About families. Ben was beginning to get a real grip on things.

No. Leaving would be stupid. He couldn't leave. Wouldn't leave. He could control this situation. He was a man, wasn't he? A tough guy. The timing was off. He wasn't finished getting his business back on its feet. No—that wasn't the primary reason. The kids. Two boys. One girl. All looked to him and Abby to provide a safe, happy, loving atmosphere for them to grow up in. For now that was the only answer. If he had to learn to keep a stranglehold on his true feelings…

True feelings. The realization washed over him in a slam like a tidal wave crossing the Atlantic. He was in love. The words nearly knocked him over. It was a hell of a time to realize that not every woman was like the one he'd been married to.

It wasn't true. Couldn't be. He'd promised himself it would never happen. No woman would get to his heart again. Hadn't he built walls with emotional bricks? Hadn't he locked the gates with protective attitudes? Why'd she have to turn out to be so damn special?

He slammed a can of tomato soup on the counter and grabbed the makings for grilled-cheese from the refrigerator and pitched them onto the counter. Dinner. That was the last thing on his mind.

The kids came bursting through the door, Katie in tow. Ben had a huge earthworm dangling from his dirty fingers.

"Look. This guy will be good for my flower bed at the store."

Jack was leaning back against the sink, a wide, smug smile on his face. This was what it was all about. "He's a juicy one, all right. Put him outside in a can and come back and wash up. Nick, take Katie up and scrub her good, will ya?"

"Okay."

Abby passed them on the stairs. She'd changed to shorts and a shirt, and her feet were bare.

"You remember I said I'd never trust a woman again?" he asked as he peeled the paper from the cheese and made a stack.

"I do."

"It seems I trust you. Otherwise, I wouldn't be handing over part of myself to you."

What a revelation. How much had it cost him to admit that? How much had it cost him to realize that? She was speechless, so she began laying the slices of bread out in a row to be buttered.

"All of us, as a unit, have lived together about seven, eight weeks now. It's working. We're a family unit. We're like a married couple but without some of the really good parts. I'm human. It's starting to get to me."

"Don't push me, Jack. I made a promise to myself. I would never, never hand my entire life over to any man again. And you being the kind of man you are, won't settle for less. I know I'm sending mixed signals to you and I'm sorry. It's just that sometimes you're so darn good to me that I forget..."

"Then maybe what I was thinking earlier might not be a bad idea."

"And what was that?"

"It's time for me to go."

"What a stupid thing to say." She hadn't considered that. And it hurt. "I never figured you for a quitter. And you're not going anywhere. You have a library book with a due date on it. You have things to do here."

She didn't want him to leave. Wouldn't let him, she knew. He had come to be too important in her life. If she had to ignore some of the strength of feeling, if she had to work hard at not caring too much, then she would do it. Whatever it took.

Neither of them noticed Ben close the screen door quietly and creep away.

Chapter Ten

When two little boys put their heads together, it can spell trouble. And it did.

Nick was deep in thought while he sat on an over-turned bucket in the yard. Ben kept bugging him. "Don't keep asking me questions right now. I have to think of something to keep Jack here. We'll go away for a while. He'll have to stay here with Mom 'cause she'll be worried."

Ben hung his head. "What did I do, Nicky?"

"Nothing, stupid. If Jack's talking about leaving already, it's...well, I don't know. But it's not you, Benny."

Benny was persistent. He wasn't quite sure they should be doing this. "How we going to get there?"

"Mom and Jack are watching us out the window. Just go play in the sandbox with Katie. I'm going in the garage to work on the wagon."

"What wagon?"

"The old one."

* * *

The breakfast dishes done, Abby stood looking out the kitchen window. "Sometimes it's the silence."

Jack looked up from his newspaper and watched Abby as she gazed out the window. "What's the silence?"

"What gets to me more than anything. After Jim died and the boys would finally be asleep. The later it got, the quieter it got. The silence. Somehow it represented the emptiness, how alone I really was caring for the kids, how scared I was."

Jack laid the newspaper down and came to stand beside Abby. Dropping a friendly arm over her shoulder, he pulled her next to him. "Everything you just said is in the past tense."

"Amazing, isn't it? The difference one human being can make in another's life. Katie is like my own daughter. I wanted one so badly. Boys are wonderful, and I wouldn't change that for the world, but a little girl can bring a mother separate things, just as sons bring something special to their fathers."

"Katie loves you, too."

"I know she does. In such a short time, she trusts me, she is completely at ease with all of us here. She has a stable family life. Something she can depend on, and somehow she knows that already."

He kissed her hand. "You've been just what she needed in her life."

Abby leaned her head back against his shoulder. "And so have you."

"I'm her father. I'm supposed to be just what she needs."

"No," she added quietly, "I mean in my life."

Abby felt his arm tighten around her, felt his lips at her temple.

She reached up and linked her fingers with his. "It's happening."

"What?" His voice was thick with emotion.

"Something unidentifiable. I'm scared now more than ever."

"I don't like to hear that. Have I let you down for one minute since we've been together?"

"Well, let's see." She laughed a little nervously. "What's it been? All of two months?"

"Look, Abby, we were just with the wrong people before. Let's face it. Maybe we shouldn't go on distrusting and waiting for the worst to happen."

"You're right." She shook her head and it rolled against his chest. "Look at those beautiful babies out there. Our marriages were suitable for the time. But that time has gone away."

"I remember being sure I loved Pat, but now that I think about it, I know I never did. I didn't know what love was. I was never this happy or content. I was out and around, busy with my business. Katie came along. We just did our thing. I guess it was right for then. So what's right for now?"

Abby sighed heavily. "I wish I knew."

It squeezed his heart. "If this manny thing is going to keep throwing us together in an emotional storm, I'll be forced to give up this job and go away."

Fury. It rolled in over her like a sandstorm on the desert. "That's just like a man. Things aren't going well—cut and run." Despite herself, her anger rose quickly. "Give me a little credit. We've been helping each other this far along. You trust me, you said so yourself. So just shut up and get on with it."

"Women! As long as I live, they'll always be a mystery."

"Do whatever you want. Men usually do anyway."

She turned out from under his arm and away from the back door.

Nick packed every piece of camping gear he could fit into the wagon and still leave room for Katie. He could carry the pup tent on his back, stuff food in the knapsack and attach that to the wooden side of the wagon. He added two flashlights to his pile of booty. And a hammer in case a snake poked its head in the tent. He'd make Jack see how important they had become to each other.

Jack sat on the front porch. The evening was sweet and mellow. He could hear Abby in the background stomping around. Up the stairs, down the stairs. Living-room light on. Then off. Doors opening, doors closing.

He couldn't ask for anything more than he had right this minute, yet it wasn't his. Not in the way he wanted it to be. What was the next step? He would do anything he had to do to make Abby happy. And Nick and Ben. His sons. That was how he thought of them now. His. And there could be a child they produced together. Another brother or sister for the kids to love.

Why did the absolute right words evade him? With circumstances the way they were now, what would happen next? Would the contentment, the peace he had come to know here, be removed from his life? Would everything change again? He wouldn't let it. Not without a fight. But he also wouldn't hurt Abby and the boys. Ever. For now, maybe, it was best to do nothing.

Inside, Abby kept herself busy strictly to keep from going out to the porch. The kids had been busy all day long outside. They were back outside again. Katie had been put to bed early after having fallen asleep on the floor playing with her dolls, her shoes filled with sand.

She knew Jack was sitting on the swing, mulling over what had happened between them. What was best to do. How to go about it.

She stopped plumping the couch pillows and stood up straight. All along they had been wrapped up in new feelings, changes, adaptations and a wariness.

Enough. No more wondering. No more guessing. No more insecurities. Caution was thrown to the wind. She was ready, willing and able to take the risk because he had taught her it wouldn't be the same. He had given her the courage to strike out, unafraid.

Taking a deep breath, Abby pushed her hair behind her ears and straightened her clothes. It was time to take charge.

Abby punched open the screen door and walked out into the growing darkness. The lilacs at the corner of the house were exploding with bloom. The scent lit the night. Fireflies darted here and there in the yard. Cars moved slowly down the street.

She marched over to the swing and dropped down in his lap.

Surprised and pleased, Jack gathered her to him. "What's this all about?"

"Nothing. Just hold me." Like any old married

woman would, she put her arms around his neck and rested her head on his shoulder.

They sat that way for a few moments while words and emotions tumbled over each other in her mind. Buying time, Abby lifted her face and placed her lips on his cheek.

"What's that for?"

Oh, if she could only explain it to him.

"For you. For being you. For being here with us. I feel like Ben's yo-yo. Back and forth. Up and down. That's right. Now it's wrong. I'm just going with it, Jack, and if you hurt me, I'll punch your lights out."

She heard his long intake of breath before he spoke the words, quietly and forcefully, into her ear. "I don't know what life holds for us. I can't promise you or the boys won't be hurt ever again, but I can promise you it won't be me that causes the pain. I do promise you we'll have each other to depend on."

The conviction in his voice, the belief in his tone, had her very close to tears. She held on to him even tighter. Her lips were at his throat.

Holding back, being careful—the time for that was over. Now it was time for truth. "Lady, will you become my wife? For real?"

She rose up and gazed into his beautiful eyes.

He lowered his mouth to hers. This time there was no crushing need, no slamming desire, only soft, sweet love. Only the refreshing knowledge of being together, and the promise of all the days and nights to come.

"I love you." He said the words slowly and with conviction. As if he'd never said them before.

"And I love you."

He stood up and picked her up, hugging her to him, swinging her around in circles.

He whispered in her ear, "I think I must have loved you from the first moment I saw you."

He set her feet on the floor. "That long ago, huh! When were you going to tell me?"

"You never wanted to hear it, but now that you have...I'm never going to stop saying it. I'm head-over-heels, no-turning-back in love with the lady Abigail Roberts...Murdock. Wait!"

His tone caused her to jump with alarm. "What now?"

"I don't have a ring," he said incredulously.

She laughed, freedom and happiness filling her voice. "I'll give you one at the ceremony."

"No, no. I mean for you. I shouldn't have proposed yet. I should have had a ring. Stay here."

Dumbfounded, Abby sat on the swing as Jack dashed back into the house and disappeared upstairs. Then she heard him run down the stairs, out the side door and open the door to his truck. He fiddled in there a minute, and then she heard the door slam. Jack sauntered around the side of the house and up onto the porch.

He stood before her. "You haven't answered my question yet."

The tears did come then, slowly sliding down her cheeks. "Of course I'll marry you. But I won't promise it'll be easy all the time."

"I don't want it any other way than it's been already. Hold out your hand."

Perplexed, she held up her hand. He took it and slid something cold and hard over her third finger. She held it up to the living-room backlight. A lock washer. How perfect. How absolutely, wonderfully flawless.

The tears came quicker now. "It's beautiful." She jumped out of the swing and into his arms.

"It's not a diamond, but that makes it official. You're wearing my ring. You're my girl. There's no getting out of it."

"I don't need a diamond. This is us. You and me." She wrapped her arms around him and held on tightly. "Let's go tell the boys."

"In a minute. I just don't want any space between us right now. This moment belongs just to us. One more minute." He kissed her cheek, beneath her ear where her scent lingered. They stood there, pressed against one another, wallowing in the newfound freedom of unconditional love.

"Okay." Jack reared back and looked down at her. "The boys are in the garage working on the old wagon. Let's go tell them." He dropped a kiss on her nose and then whispered in her ear as they started back through the house, "Mrs. Murdock."

The garage light was on, but when they reached the doors they found no children.

Abby sighed. "Nick? Ben? Where'd you go? They must be upstairs. They just forgot to turn out the light and shut the doors. Typical."

They started back into the night. There, near the switch, nailed to the wall, was a piece of notebook paper with words penciled on it.

We don't want Jack to leave. We are safe. Don't be mad at us. We have food.

P.S. We want Jack to be our dad.

"Lordy." Jack leaned heavily against the wall. "They must have overheard me talking to you earlier about leaving. How stupid can I get?"

"Stop it, Jack. If you start blaming yourself, I'll have to take my first steps as your intended and knock some sense into you."

"Well, that's plain enough."

Abby's voice was filled with amusement. "They can't have Katie. I put her to bed myself."

Together they raced through the house and into Katie's room. She was gone, and so was her floppy-eared gray rabbit that she slept with.

"If anything happens to those kids..."

In her brain, Abby knew Nick was a capable child. He wouldn't do anything foolish enough to endanger any of them. In her heart, she prayed she was right.

Speaking with more bravado than she felt, and hiding her real fears, she slipped her hand in his. "They'll be fine. Nick is mature for his age. He knows the dangers out there. Let's think. Where could they have gone? Not far toting Katie and her rabbit, that's for sure."

"The wagon. Was it out there?"

They ran back to the garage.

"It's gone. So that's why Nick was so interested in repairing it this evening. Slick little devil even got me to help him tighten the wheels. I should be more careful about what I say when the kids could hear me."

Abby was over in a corner rummaging around. "So it's a learning experience for you. Settle down. And their tent is gone. The cooking gear. I'll bet when we look, their sleeping bags are gone. They're camping somewhere. Close by, you can bet. Nemo! Nemo!''

When no yipping, bouncing mongrel made an appearance, Abby concluded, ''And they took him, too. God, this is like something on 'Little House on the Prairie.' Maybe Mr. Edwards will come dragging over the field with the kids on his back.''

''Your attempt at humor is lost on me at this moment. Let's call the police.''

''Jack. I know you're scared senseless about Katie. I acted like a lunatic when Ben wandered off and I am concerned, but I don't think the kids are far. Can we look for them ourselves first?''

He held his hands up. ''You're right. Where do we start? I can't think straight.''

Abby thought a minute. ''Behind the school and then the park. They can reach both places pulling the wagon.''

''Let's go.''

Abby ran to the kitchen to get her keys. ''I have a spotlight in the van, we'll take that.''

Behind the school was dark and deserted. They drove the van slowly over every inch of it. The park was next.

At first look, they found nothing. Pulling away, Abby caught sight of a floppy-tailed mongrel puppy happily loping their way. Relief flooded through her. She hadn't realized how uptight she really was. She grabbed hold of Jack's shirt.

''Look over there. Here comes Nemo. Won't the boys be upset that he gave them away? He's dragging his leash behind him. They're here somewhere.''

Jack scrubbed his hands over his face. And then

turned in the seat to kiss Abby smack on the mouth. "Thank God. I hope they're all right. You're one heck of a mother."

She laughed. "And you, being the father of three, aren't so bad yourself."

They parked the van and climbed out, Nemo jumping up for affection.

"Nick," Abby shouted.

"Ben," Jack yelled.

"Come on, boys, we have Nemo. We know you're out here. We're not angry," Abby tried again, venturing out into the darkness, directionless.

Silence. Nothing. Abby looked back at Jack and saw honest, cold fear dull his eyes.

"Relax, Jack. They're okay. Go get Nicky, Nemo," Abby ordered.

The dog sat on his haunches, tongue lolling out to the side, and looked blankly at them.

Abby took Jack by the hand. She was more confident than he was that the kids were fine. "Let's drive a little closer to the woods and use the light again."

The little tent was pitched just inside the thicket. It stood crookedly and was on a slight incline, but it was tied securely to a sapling. A dim light was glowing from the inside. The boys had done a pretty good job of camouflaging it and the wagon with twigs and branches. A log was set up outside the tent with their cooking utensils lined up on it. The wagon held firewood they had gathered.

"They were serious."

Abby snickered. "What did you think? Those kids aren't about to let you out of their lives."

Jack and Abby approached the little fortress. Kneeling down and pulling the flap of the tent back, picking up the quickly failing flashlight that had been left on, Jack shone it on the faces of the three sleeping children and one gray rabbit.

"God protects little kids and old raggedy stuffed rabbits," Jack said, and exchanged relieved looks with Abby. She rested her head in the crook of his arm. They took some time to simply be glad the kids were okay.

Abby took Jack's hand and pulled him to stand beside her. "Everything's going to be all right now, Jack. Nothing and nobody can beat the five of us together." Right there, standing together in the darkness, the resolution was made.

A few minutes later, Jack shook Nick gently. Nick rolled over slowly, and then his eyes flew open.

"Am I in trouble?"

Abby and Jack laughed. They couldn't help it. The tension of the past hours slipped away. Together they gathered Nick in a huge hug.

"No, Nicky, you're not. Your mother and I just decided to come camping with you."

"Guess I didn't hide as good as I thought I did."

"Oh, I don't know. It was a pretty good job. Anyone else might not have found you, but your parents…well, they have a sense about things like this."

"My parents?"

Jack was grinning from ear to ear. "Yes. Your mother agreed to marry me tonight. That is, if it's okay with you kids."

"Wow," Nick said with wonder in his voice. He jumped and shot a hand toward the sky. "Radical."

Abby squeezed her arms around Jack's waist and kissed his shoulder. "I think that means he's pleased."

Nick moved over and flung his arms around the two of them. "Mom and...and Dad."

The three of them clung to each other for a long few minutes. The night air was filled with the aura of unification. Of victory. Of eternity.

Jack moved over to the dying fire, breaking twigs and branches and blowing on the flames. Abby sat on the ground, Nemo next to her, and just watched Jack handle this one.

"Ben said you were leaving. He was afraid it was because of him. Us."

"Not ever. Your mother and I were both scared of facing what we felt for each other. What I was talking about was having to leave rather than hurt her. But she decided to keep me. She said I can stay."

Nick's grin was wide as he looked up at Abby. "Mom's a pretty smart lady."

At that moment, Abby saw some of Jim in her son, and for the first time it didn't sear through her; it just made her proud.

Nick jumped Jack. Together they rolled across the grass, wrestling. "We can wake up Benny and Katie now and go home."

"I thought you wanted a night of camping. Your mother and I can stay out here, too. Did you bring hot dogs? I'm starving."

"No. But maybe if we asked Mom real nice, she would go back to the house and get some stuff...."

If the truth be told, Abby didn't want to move a muscle, but she stood up and turned for the van.

Just then, Ben came powering out of the tent, fright written all over his face. When he saw Abby and Jack, he looked to Nick for assurance that they weren't in deep trouble.

"It's okay now, Benny. Jack's not going to leave. He's going to be our other dad."

Both children's faces looked toward Jack, where the flames were now beginning to leap and dance, shooting sparks up into the dark sky.

Jack took Abby's hand and waited for Ben's reaction. When Ben broke and ran to him, throwing both little arms around his knees, they were both so happy.

Another commotion was heard coming from the tent area. "Emo. Emo. Bad Emo."

All of them turned toward the tent and watched as Katie toddled out, her pajama bottoms twisted as Nemo tried to pull her back into the tent with his teeth.

Family laughter followed the sparks high into the night sky.

Jack moved to Katie and rescued her from Nemo's overzealous protection. Hoisting her on his shoulders, he watched as the boys danced wildly around him and the campfire. Shadows zigzagged along the ground. The dog plopped down in the entrance to the pup tent and watched all this monkey business, his muzzle resting comfortably on his crossed front paws.

It was a perfect family scene. It was a promise of all the wonderful days ahead.

"Well, soon-to-be Mrs. Murdock, are you going back to the house and get the hot dogs or what?"

"Ketchup, too, Mom. We couldn't bring all the good stuff."

She stepped up into the van and looked back. Her brood. She had it all now. Everything.

Jack, Katie still on his shoulders, her little hands plastered on his forehead, walked over to her and placed a kiss on her lips. Dipping down so Katie was lower, she received her kiss from Abby.

Jack stood tall again. "Don't be long, Mom. Your family is waiting for you."

*   *   *   *   *

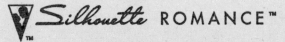

IN CELEBRATION OF MOTHER'S DAY, JOIN
SILHOUETTE THIS MAY AS WE BRING YOU

a funny thing
HAPPENED ON THE WAY TO THE
DELIVERY Room

THESE THREE STORIES, CELEBRATING THE
LIGHTER SIDE OF MOTHERHOOD, ARE
WRITTEN BY YOUR FAVORITE AUTHORS:

KASEY MICHAELS
KATHLEEN EAGLE
EMILIE RICHARDS

When three couples make the trip to the delivery
room, they get more than their own bundles of
joy...they get the promise of love!

Available this May,
wherever Silhouette books are sold.

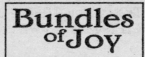

Bundles of Joy

The biggest romantic surprises come in the smallest packages!

January:

HAVING GABRIEL'S BABY by Kristin Morgan (#1199)
After one night of passion Joelle was expecting! The dad-to-be, rancher Gabriel Lafleur, insisted on marriage. But could they find true love as a family?

April:

YOUR BABY OR MINE? by Marie Ferrarella (#1216)
Single daddy Alec Beckett needed help with his infant daughter! When the lovely Marissa Rogers took the job with an infant of her own, Alec realized he wanted this mom-for-hire *permanently*—as part of a real family!

Don't miss these irresistible Bundles of Joy, coming to you in January and April, only from

Silhouette ROMANCE™

In the tradition of
Anne Rice comes a
daring, darkly sensual
vampire novel by

As a bonus,
you will also receive
a FREE story by
National Bestselling Author
Stella Cameron,
in the same volume.

MAGGIE SHAYNE

BORN IN TWILIGHT

Rendezvous hails bestselling Maggie Shayne's vampire
romance series, WINGS IN THE NIGHT, as
"powerful...riveting...unique...intensely romantic."

Don't miss it, this March, available
wherever Silhouette books are sold.

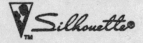

Silhouette®

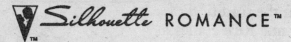
Silhouette ROMANCE™

cordially invites you to the unplanned nuptials
of three unsuspecting hunks and their

**SURPRISE
BRIDES**

Look for the following specially packaged titles:

March 1997: MISSING: ONE BRIDE by Alice Sharpe, #1212
April 1997: LOOK-ALIKE BRIDE by Laura Anthony, #1220
May 1997: THE SECRET GROOM by Myrna Mackenzie, #1225

Don't miss **Surprise Brides,** an irresistible trio of books about love
and marriage by three talented authors! Found only in—

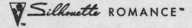
Silhouette ROMANCE™